SPIRITUAL INTRUDERS
The Just Shall Live By Faith

Brenda Murphy

This book is dedicated to those who will stand in faith:
Believing that God is a keeper of His Word and promises.
Looking to Him for all their needs to be supplied no matter the
situation, circumstances or testing.
Choosing to trust God's impeccable timing in their lives.
Believing that our God never, ever fails!

Always Count That Day
Poet Catherine Pulsifer, © 2012
(used by permission)

As we age we realize that,
Our days on earth are few.
And with that thought we start to think,
There were days we just ran through.

These were usually days gone fast,
Because they weren't much fun.
And when we look back in our thoughts,
These days are often gone.

Wasted days are not so good,
Especially when we have so few.
Even days that aren't so good,
Are days I have with you.

So from now on my attitude will change,
And I will count that day.
The days of good, the days of bad,
Will all be my days array.

I will count that day no matter what,
And I will always remember it.
Life is too short as it is,
And this I will admit.

No more will I skip a day,
Or erase it from my mind.
I'll take each moment of each day,
And be thankful and kind.

Contents

Acknowledgements

With all sincerity, I would like to thank my publisher, Lisa Bell, who believed in my writings and read multiple versions of my book stories with immense thoughtfulness and generosity. Over the years, Lisa has dedicated countless of hours to editing draft after draft of my books, and this one is no exception.

Not only did Lisa do the editing of the manuscript for *Spiritual Intruders*, she also provided meaningful feedback that served as the catalyst for me to move forward with publication. In the very beginning of my writings, when I was looking for someone to publish my books, Lisa and I started out as merely publisher and writer, but along the way, Lisa has become one of my greatest encouragers, writing mentors and friend. For that, I am very grateful.

I would also like to give special thanks to Rick Schroeppel, my book cover designer. I am very blessed and fortunate to have the artistry of Rick's designs as a personal cover on several of my published books such as *Raw Faith, Living In Purpose, Cycles, Forgetting the Former Things* and now, *Spiritual Intruders*. Thank you Rick for putting your heart and soul and your personal uniqueness into every book cover design you created for me. Your work always manages to express the heartbeat of what I am writing.

Lastly, I would like to publicly thank everyone who has ever read, purchased or supported me in any way toward helping my books become realized, written, and published. Your love, generosity and genuine support of my work has been the necessary fuel that propels me to reach for higher inspiration and greater desires.

Sincerely,

Brenda

in·trud·er

[inˈtroōdər]
NOUN

Intruders (plural noun)

A person who intrudes, especially into a building with
criminal intent.
To thrust oneself in without invitation, permission, or
welcome. To enter as a geological intrusion. To thrust or
force in or upon someone or something especially without
permission, welcome, or fitness intruder himself into their
lives. To cause to enter as if by force.

Part One

"When you say, 'I can't' and expect the worst to happen, you close the doors to the land of success and accomplishment."

~Author Unknown~

At a Glance, Second Glancing

This book is dedicated to the individuals who always believed if they invested in enough safety devices, hired private security, purchased the latest upscale dead-bolt locks, placed fancy security bars on their windows and doors; purchased the latest "must have" elaborate alarm system, or succumbed to the pressure of buying a firearm or getting a vicious dog or a pet to keep them company day and night, then they could escape the perils lurking deep within their hearts.

They thought investing in such things would somehow provide the level of comfort, protection and soundness of mind they needed to be safe, sheltered from the bad people who would never get inside to hurt them.

Those who spend their entire savings for what they believe buys peace of mind for a lifetime might very well be surprised in the end. The enemy they feared could quite possibly be the one inside, piercing through the scope of their own illicit thoughts.

The ability to feel safe in their homes and surroundings or places of business could cost them everything, depending upon personal perspective.

For these individuals, the one-million dollar question remains. "Could it be possible the enemy they wholeheartedly believe lives outside the realm and scope of who they were created to be somehow is the same one who lurks from within?" That enemy merely exists from a different viewpoint.

Perhaps the true peace and security they spent thousands of dollars obtaining, desperately believing that "No weapon formed against them would truly prosper." Never once giving thought that perhaps the true enemy they warred against did not live on the outer scope of who they believed they were. On the contrary, that enemy lived on the inside, contradicting who they subconsciously thought they were.

Remember, "For as he thinketh in his heart, so is he: Eat and drink, saith he to thee; but his heart is not with thee." (Proverbs 23:7 KJV)

"For he is the kind of man who is always thinking about the cost. 'Eat and drink,' he says to you, but his heart is not with you." (Proverbs 23:7 NIV)

Introduction

Have you ever met someone, introduced or by chance, and in that particular moment during the introduction, you suddenly felt as though you knew them from somewhere else? Perhaps you met them before in a certain place or at an event?

Have you ever noticed or had a moment when you caught the gaze of someone across the room, and their timing of looking at you ran parallel to you staring or gazing at them? For a moment, it seemed as though they "knew" you, or at the very least, they could see right through you. Suddenly, you sheepishly turned away, hoping that he or she didn't pick up on the vibe.

How many times have you reached your hand out to shake someone else's hand, and it left you feeling unsure whether you should have made that gesture in the first place?

Something unnerving about the touch of his or her hand left you feeling uneasy about the connection. You could not put your finger on why you felt that way. Somehow though, at the moment, you left feeling something was off about it, so you simply walked away from the encounter and dismissed the thought altogether.

Lastly, have you ever been out and about and thought you saw someone in the crowd you recognized? You called his or her name or even chased after that one because you were so sure the person you saw from a distance was who you thought for sure you knew.

You wondered to yourself why your acquaintance didn't acknowledge you. Why did he or she pretend not to know you or ignored you altogether?

Determined not to let this moment go, you rushed to catch up and force him or her to say hello. However, when the individual turned to look back, you realized you made a serious mistake. You really had no knowledge of that person at all?

Interestingly enough, here you are following in hot pursuit behind someone you would have bet your life on knowing when, in fact, you were dead wrong.

In all honestly, when he or she turned around, it wasn't that familiar person at all. Not only did he or she appear surprised that you followed and touched a shoulder with such confidence. The individual was curious why you thought he or she was someone else in the first place. Feeling embarrassed, you apologized profusely and sped off the other direction.

Likewise, have you ever encountered a certain vibe or spiritual presence when you entered a room? The atmosphere appeared to be light, joyful and jovial when you first entered. Shortly thereafter, you felt as though you walked in on a subject matter about you—whether good, bad or indifferent.

You sensed a strong shift in the midst of it all. Right where you stood, there was a sense of walking into something that felt as if you didn't really belong. Maybe you should not be there in the first place.

Wait, don't tell me—you stayed, anyway. Despite the gut-wrenching emotion of leave now before you regret it, you stayed feeling. Or you talked yourself out of that warning and shrugged it off as being silly and decided to stay after all. Denouncing the fact that everything within you screamed, "Get out! You don't fit in this moment." Call it pride or what have you, but against your better judgment, you convinced yourself to stay instead.

Believe it or not, there are so many missed opportunities where certain signs or clues are given to us as life lessons. But most of us simply dismiss the thought, the moment, the intention and sometimes even the blatant perspective of what's happening right before our eyes.

We would rather tell ourselves that everything is alright than accept the fact something may be amiss or awry, and we need to pay close attention to what's happening right before our eyes.

Have you ever been away from home, and to the best of your knowledge, everything was fine when you left. You checked and even double checked to make sure all the windows and doors were locked. The stove was turned off, and you were confident everything was in its rightful place.

You arrived at work safely. So far, you were having a regular work day, getting things done according to your schedule. Suddenly, you sensed a real need to call or go home immediately.

You thought, "Why? There is no real need to worry, I just checked on the family a few minutes ago, and everything was well. I am sure it isn't anything to concern myself with. Besides, I will call later on my break just to check in."

Hours went by, and when you finally surrendered to that little quiet, still voice, not only were you glad you did, but you were shocked at how you were forewarned about the possible situation. But you overrode your conscience to follow through only to find out it was a true emergency after all.

Spiritual Intruders is a book about second guessing ourselves when we don't fully understand what our thoughts are trying to forewarn or alert us about. It's about trying to figure things out on our own without the aid and total dependence upon God who knows all.

It's about understanding that God loves and values us as His children and that He wants the very best for us at all times. There is never a lapse in time when He leaves or abandons us. God's ways and heart toward us are perfect because He is a perfect God.

Being mindful of Spiritual Intruders can serve as a spiritual wake-up call if only we are willing to lean in closer to the voice of God and stay focused on and avoid the pitfalls clearly outlined for us in the Word of God.

For instance, have you ever thought about why Halloween is considered a well-celebrated "holiday" or event for all children and sadly for a whole lot of adults?

Most of the children who come trick-or-treating at our doors on Halloween night will be dressed as princesses and super heroes. According to statistics, those are the most popular costumes. There will be others who will push the envelope much further to more unimaginable attire as their heroes or favorites.

From the time I was very young, I always heard Halloween being referred to as Satan's holiday. That bright red, fork-tailed, pointy-eared devil costume will not be a preferred sight to look at whether on Halloween or not.

Still, it's amazing how readily the world makes an

exception for that one day worldwide but declare days afterward they don't believe in the devil himself.

Wouldn't it be nice, though, if the devil really did wear a bright red suit with noticeable horns and signage that stated right out-of-the-box who he really was and his intentions to kill, steal and destroy those he came into contact with? We might find it easier to spot him and put up our guard.

For Eve, he took the form of a serpent (Genesis 3:4). An interesting choice. Serpents are noxious creatures that creep stealthily, hiss menacingly, and inject poison into their victims.

Need we say more about the similarities between Satan and serpents? It reminds me of how easily Spiritual Intruders enter our thought patterns, thoughts and how we interpret things we entertain.

If you desire a clearer definition of our enemy, he's called the evil one in Matthew 13:19. Look up evil in the dictionary and his character is clearly described: morally reprehensible, wicked, offensive, causing harm, bringing sorrow, distress and calamity.

Satan is our enemy (1 Peter 5:8). He seeks to injure, overthrow, and confound us. He is a harmful and deadly opponent, hostile, and filled with ill will.

Daily, he challenges us to submit to our fears, doubts and woes over faith, belief and confidence in God, even when the evidence points glaringly to the obvious that turning right is the only conceivable choice to make.

Sometimes, in those critical moments, in that last ditch effort, we are still prone to go down the road of least resistance because it appears to be safe, if not familiar. It's the one of least resistance and minimal effort or pushback.

Let's remember that Spiritual Intruders are those inward, sabotaging thoughts and derailments that come from the inner enemy's design to thwart the progress God planned for our lives—for right now as well as in the near and long-term future. We must not be afraid to dream big and reach for the unimaginable things that we believe God for in our lives.

Have you ever experienced moments when you made up your mind to throw caution to the wind and totally depend upon God, casting fear and doubt to the side?

Instantly, in those moments, the enemy wants us to second guess ourselves. Believe it or not, he will also bring about direct conflict through others who only days, weeks, months or even years ago were your greatest supporters and champions.

Now, they have seemingly turned their backs on you as if they never honestly thought you could accomplish the goal in the first place.

Let's take a look at 1 Peter 5:8. In this verse, Peter says, "The devil prowls around like a roaring lion looking for someone to devour." (NLT) He reminds us lions attack sick, young, and straggling animals. And Satan does the same.

The enemy realizes that, as believers, we are sometimes at our weakest defense when we are suffering, depressed, or being persecuted. That's when he loves to move in for the kill. And he often chooses a time when we're alone and more easily swayed.

The devil is our accuser (Revelation 12:10). First, he lies to us, trying to convince us that whatever he's suggesting will make us happy. Then he turns around and uses our sins to accuse us of disobedience and unfaithfulness before God! In fact, in the Hebrew language, the name Satan means accuser.

Not fully understanding that our greatest life lessons or treasures can often be found in our intangibles. They are the life lessons that one can only learn through our personal experiences and seeing a thing, situation or circumstance through to the end.

The enemy is extremely mindful that keeping us second guessing threatens to keep you and me in the dark, blindsided, and in ignorance of what, where, how, why and when to move or if to move at all.

He spends all his time bombarding our thoughts with negativity, cloudy judgment, unresolved issues and misconstrued ideology about matters that have nothing to do with the future.

This is when we need to trust, rest and rely upon God more. Only He knows the challenges that are anywhere from zero to 20 years ahead in our journey. And He alone has a plan to see us through every conceivable obstacle. We need to be settled in the fact that God is and will always be pro-us. In Him alone, we are all winners.

However, if we choose to stall and act on a second guess, if we abort today's mission, we will be inadequately prepared for future accomplishments and will most likely spend time repeating the learned experience multiple times.

In addition, second guessing ourselves causes us to deny God the opportunity to perform miracles and intended purposes for our lives.

Think back to a time when you made an "executive" decision without prayer, guidance, thought or even reason. You dove in emotions first, feelings next and discovered the decision you made turned into a total nightmare because you left out the main ingredient, wisdom.

Not only was it a total nightmare, but seemingly, for every step you took forward, there were five steps backward. I mean that is fine if you're practicing how to do the "Electric Slide" or something. But not in traveling through life.

As we move forward in learning more about Spiritual Intruders, we will discover that not every horrible situation or decision we make results from bad decision-making— look at the life of Joseph, for instance.

Sometimes, God sends us a *special invitation to witness a miracle.* Don't spend your life constantly second guessing your life or decision making. Instead, let's learn how to follow through and trust that the Coach, the Author of your faith, will cause you to finish strong for the win!

The purpose of *Spiritual Intruders* is another means of looking at how to become more aware and mindful of second guessing ourselves. Spiritual Intruders can slow the progress and process toward our real goal for the plans God has for us, leading to misalignment.

When we're on our mission and purpose in life, we cannot be effective, alert, and observant by wasting time second guessing our current position, status, circumstances or situation. We must trust God and flourish right where we are, not the 1,000,000 places you *maybe-perhaps-probably could've been.*

Often the real goal is just a few steps from where you are now. We cannot see because we sometimes block personal progress even if the goal lies within close proximity. According to Philippians 3:14, we must maintain our purposed pace with proper focus and a forward press, not a backward march.

Second guessing causes us to reject the gift of contentment which is surrounded by serenity, gladness and satisfaction. There's a life treasure for all of us called *contentment*. Some of us spend a ton of energy second guessing because we have not learned how to be grateful for what we have right in front of us and how far we've come today.

Sure, it's great to aspire for more, but there is *peaceful contentment* in not being overly influenced by *what others have or are doing*, which leads us to second guess where WE are currently.

The enemy loves to cause our emotions to flutter and be filled to the brim with regret, hatred, hostility and even judgment over what others possess. In the end, it really doesn't matter how they got it, are sustaining it or even handling it. The circumstances of others are none of our business in the first place.

Sometimes we don't need more; we don't need to move left, right, or back—we're just fine where WE are at this moment. Choosing to be still and know that God has you where you are currently is a major consolation prize that is not always easy to win. But we must be willing to keep on trying.

Second guessing immobilizes you while you attempt to predict the future. It's called a second **"guess"** for a reason. No amount of time or energy pouring over the facts (as you know them today) will guarantee that you will predict an accurate, alternate, better future than what God already purposed for your life.

It doesn't matter how hard we work in our own strength.

It will never override the plans of God for our destiny. When God created us, He didn't simply "willy-nilly" us together. No, He had an authentic and legitimate plan for our days here on earth.

If we were that good, we'd never need a **SECOND** guess—our **FIRST** guess would be on point! So as you sit there ruminating, over-analyzing, and peering into your crystal ball of personal thoughts, you're stagnant. You're stuck.

Release yourself from the second-guessing-trap, put away your crystal ball, meaning your perspective, ideas, motives and rehearsed answers. Decide you are going to trust God with the schematics of the blueprint for your life and total destiny, and keep moving forward to find the life treasures God already purposed for you to discover.

Remember, when second guessing comes to state its claim on our victories, it leads us in surrender to a poverty-stricken mindset. With those thoughts, we can never conquer debt or even remotely become debt free, let alone pay our debt from month-to-month. We cannot come into agreement or allow our faith to grab hold of such a belief. Otherwise, we cannot possibly see ourselves ever being rid of such bondage.

In fact, for some, the closer we become to being debt free, the more unrealistic and scary it all seems. The cloud of bondage that debt has carried over our mindset for so long keeps us from the possibility of reaching that goal. Changing our thought process can become quite daunting and overwhelming within itself.

Whatever our personal goals and dreams, going forward, let's make up our minds to make success a "*lifestyle*." For example, losing weight and keeping it off becomes a new weight loss "*lifestyle*" as opposed to losing weight only to fit into a new outfit or win the approval of someone else without making it a personal goal.

Without the lifestyle mindset, we too easily self-destruct and return to the old-mindset. After all, if the goal is for the wrong reasons, and if the goal was distorted from the beginning, it will not be sustainable.

As we move into the heartbeat of *Spiritual Intruders*, we find a fiction story about a smart, intelligent, highly motivated, energetic business woman who secretly desired to one day become a world renowned jetsetter in all she put her mind and hand too.

Her name is Meredith, and she believed if she worked hard enough and paid her dues of getting a stellar education, accompanied by sought after degrees, awards, fellowships and honorable mentions, she could one day rub elbows with the world's rich and famous. Who knows—maybe even become one herself, having an extravagant lifestyle in comparison to others in her close-knit circle.

At that particular time in life, she was willing to do whatever she had to, within reason, to make sure it happened on her Rolex watch.

Part Two

"Happiness comes of the capacity to feel deeply,
to enjoy simply, to think freely, to risk life,
to be needed."

~Storm Jameson~

*"Be not forgetful to entertain strangers: for thereby
some have entertained angels unawares."*
~Hebrews 13:2 KJV

Guests Unawares

As a young girl, Meredith was a beautiful, charming, smart and witty individual. Early on, it was easy to see that she excelled in pretty much anything she put her hands to. Sharp, fast learner, adaptable to change, eager and headstrong to boot, everyone loved Meredith because she was easy to talk to and easy to love.

All through high school and her college years, Meredith kept her head down, focusing on goals, her hopes and dreams within arm's reach. She wholeheartedly believed that one day she would become the CEO of her own mentoring company with multitudes of loyal employees—and even more clients.

From the early days of college and even after graduate school, Meredith worked tirelessly to bring her dreams into alignment with hopes for future endeavors.

She very rarely took any time off for herself to enjoy the fruits of her labor. She figured there would be plenty of time to do that one day. However, today would not be the day to start.

On most occasions, if she wasn't working at her office, she was making dreams happen for others in various capacities. Meredith recognized the level of confidence, hope, tenacity and drive it took to make one's dreams a reality, so she always instilled in others to never, ever give up. No matter what.

Meredith always dreamed of living what she called the "Jet-Set" lifestyle. In her mind, the idea of jet setting was a term known in the world of journalism—an international social group of wealthy people who travelled the world to participate in social activities unavailable to ordinary people.

The term which replaced café society, came from the lifestyle of travelling from one stylish or exotic place to another via private jet planes.

All her adult life, Meredith bought into thinking that at some point in life, you fall into a rut. Maybe you've been doing the same career for years, and it's no longer exciting or challenging. Maybe you love your career, but have no life outside work. Maybe you just feel lost in general about what your future may hold in the long run.

She also believed if you want to do better, you must change your perspective about how you see yourself and recreate the space around you to fit that new, improved image. For Meredith, the following scenarios applied.

To achieve her new goals, which was to become a jetsetter and live the lifestyle she always dreamed, she needed to take her life to the next level. To realize that, she needed to raise her standards across the board—not just to work hard, but play hard too.

She believed raising her standards was the only thing that would create these lasting changes to her lifestyle. Raising her standards required a change to her mindset.

Uncovering her limiting beliefs would also assist her in identifying the things holding her back from being successful. She theorized that in order to change those limiting beliefs, she must change her mindset.

She understood early in her career that she must take personal responsibility for her current status and problems in order to create a solution for those matters she would encounter later in her life. More importantly, Meredith learned a critical truth—who you surround yourself with, you will become.

She concluded, "If I want success, surround myself with successful people."

Equally important to the equation—become aware of what you do, how you think and what actions you are taking. Be purposeful with your actions and thoughts.

Fast forward. After investing five long years of hard work and admiral dedication into making her business a success, Meredith decided it was time to reward herself. She actually scheduled a two-week, uninterrupted vacation. Free from work-related issues, minus a few tweaks here and there.

Prior to her scheduled vacation, she contacted some old friends from back home about getting together for girl chat and a few days of relaxation. With those plans in the works, Meredith finalized plans with her girlfriends around her time off.

On her first day of vacation, Meredith spent the morning frantically getting her house in order before her friends arrived within a couple of days. She hadn't seen them in years and missed them very much.

The first thing Meredith noticed during the first day off was how absolutely amazing the sunrise was to behold from her kitchen window.

She was astonished at the little things she missed while keeping her head down, working hard and furious to make a life for herself. Not to mention providing a nice little nest egg when she retired. Still, Meredith could not get pass how wonderfully her day was shaping up.

In the moment, Meredith decided to make herself a nice, enjoyable cup of coffee, sit outside on the patio and breathe in the gorgeous sunrise as her day gradually unfolded before her eyes.

At the outset, she planned to work smarter, not harder. When the time came, she wanted to enjoy her vacation with friends, not spend the time together running around with an over-the-top agenda. She wanted to share the moments of success and fruits of her labor with those she felt close to.

As the day progressed for Meredith, she found her workload around her household to be productive. After all, she had a plan. Around 10:00 a.m., Meredith realized so far, so good. Her plan was working, and she could honestly report that she had made major progress on all the things she had in mind to accomplish.

Meredith thought she was nearing the end of her household chores. Until she stepped into her laundry room. She realized the uphill journey had barely begun.

"Bomber," she thought to herself.

Still, on that gorgeous day, Meredith found herself so preoccupied with her around-the-house to-do list that she became overwhelmed by what she now considered urgent. The necessary things on her list could not wait for another time to be completed.

She said out loud, *"Oh my goodness where do I go from here? What is going to be first? The loads of laundry that are way overdue, or should I start the process of cleaning the oven?"*

Honestly, she didn't want to do either. While Meredith

was excellent at her career, she wasn't the neatest housekeeper in the world.

Meredith took a deep breath and exhaled slowly, realizing that no matter what, she would have to reserve enough energy to get the entire job done sooner rather than later. After all, she was expecting guests to arrive later in the week, and she wanted everything to be spot on upon her guests' arrivals.

So she put on her favorite music, turned up the dial, gathered up all her cleaning supplies, and made a party of time spent getting her house in order for her special guests. During the visit, she preferred to spend time with them rather than being preoccupied while they were there.

Becoming so carried away by the music and the beauty of the day, Meredith wasn't paying close attention to any outside distractions or time. She certainly didn't notice anything odd happening in the neighborhood. Being home during the day was not her norm, so she was in her own zone.

Late into the evening, while Meredith continued to clean and get organized, an unusual rapid knock at the front door intruded on her cleaning. At first she didn't pay attention. She barely heard the knock anyway because of the loud music, and with so much to finish, she kept cleaning.

Within a few minutes, the knock escalated to both a louder, frantic banging and the doorbell ringing at the same time. The sudden change caught Meredith's attention.

After being scared out of her wits because of the unexpected guest, Meredith realized someone at the door pounded with a sense of urgency. She needed to see who. Someone might need serious help. And she could assist them, although not sure exactly how.

On her way to the front door, Meredith continued to get a sinking feeling deep down in the pit of her stomach. Too much to simply ignore.

While she sensed that the voice was telling her something of importance; somehow, despite it all, she still felt compel to continue to move forward, anyway.

Meredith admittedly being frightened ignored her fear and reached for the door knob but decided at the last minute to look out of the peep hole instead. Next, she sensed a voice within her telling her more loudly this time, don't open that door!

She thought, "Surely this isn't the guests I expected to arrive in another 48 hours, suddenly showing up."

They would have called first to let her know their plans changed, and they were in town earlier and couldn't wait to get together. She was very confused and unnerved.

Not sure what to do, Meredith convinced herself it was a mistake of some sort. Instead, she said to herself, "Oh, it's probably no big deal. After all, it could be the paperboy, pizza guy bringing pizza to the wrong address and perhaps in a hurry. I mean, everyone makes a mistake now and then right? That's all there is too it. No need to panic."

Still, the nervousness in her stomach persisted and even greater caution set in.

Once again, the voice grew even louder. ***"Don't open that door!"***

Meredith, standing by the front door and looking through the peephole, realized she couldn't identify the person at the door who stood entirely too close to identify properly.

So she asked. "Hello, who's there? How Can I help you? Hello…"

No response was given back to her.

She asked again, "H-e-l-l-o, who's there? How can I help you?"

Still no response, but she could still sense an urgency to get in from the other side of the door. Almost in a panicky state, Meredith decided to step away from the door and look out the window instead.

Even after doing so, she still could not identify the person at the door because the individual deliberately kept his back to the window. Frustrated and angry, her pulse raced, her nerves frazzled and her knees shaky.

She once again stood back away from the door and took a deep breath. Putting on her big girl's voice, she asked again but a little more forceful.

"I said, who is it, and what do you want? If you don't tell me your name and what you want, I am going to call the police, do you hear me?"

Suddenly, the rapid knocking and ringing of the doorbell intensified.

This caused Meredith to shrink in fear, sweating profusely and totally scared out of her mind. She had forgotten her music was still playing loudly and for a brief moment thought, "Oh, that's why they cannot hear me, because I left the music playing. Silly me."

Encouraging herself that this was the real reason the person on the other side of the door could not hear her, she quickly ran back to the radio and turned it off.

Temporarily confident the matter had been resolved, she approached the door—this time with renewed assurance.

Meredith apologized to the unknown guest on the other side of the door. "I'm sorry, I forgot I had my radio on. Now would you please tell me who you are and how I can help you?"

After an awkward pause, there was still no response. Again, only a sense of urgency and agitation from the other side to have the request honored. It appeared the unwanted guest was willing to wait Meredith out, no matter how long it took.

By then, Meredith was exasperated because she couldn't understand why someone would be ringing her doorbell and knocking on her door with such urgency, yet he wouldn't respond to her questions.

What did he want? Why was he there to begin with? Meredith desperately wanted answers to those questions.

She thought, "It's the middle of the night—this can't be right. Something's wrong with this picture. I don't see a car, I didn't order anything to eat. I can't identify the person knocking and ringing the doorbell. What is really going on?" She took a deep breath. "After all, who would just stop by my house, unannounced, knocking and ringing my doorbell uncontrollably like this?" Meredith was desperately searching for answers.

As more and more time passed, Meredith was beginning to put two and two together, coming up with answers to her concern. Meredith realized this moment spelled trouble, and she needed to get help right away.

Still determined to be in control, Meredith decided she would give it another go. Once again, she put her big girl voice on and asked in confidence with forcefulness, "Who is it?"

From the other side of the door came utter silence with a twist of dread and foreboding. Again, Meredith asked—a little louder. "I said, who are you?"

Not only did silence scream from the other side of the door, the once fierce ringing and rapid knocking stopped abruptly.

Meredith, acting on pure adrenaline, responded more aggressively, spurred by the quiet. "What do you want? If you don't tell me, I am going to call the police. Do you hear me?"

Suddenly, the person outside uttered an inaudible sound, low and cryptic. Meredith could not understand, but at least she was getting to the bottom of this craziness once and for all.

Meredith decided to look out the peephole and double-check outside by looking out the front window—just to be on the safe side before opening the door.

"After all," she thought to herself, "why am I scared? I live in a good neighborhood where everyone is friendly and gets along." At least that's what she convinced herself of.

While looking out the peephole and front window, Meredith could only see the backside of a person standing on her front porch. Still unable to identify him, and against her better judgment, she slowly opened the door a crack.

At the precise moment Meredith decided to override her fears and sound judgment, she sensed the man trying to force his way into her home, life and private domain without her expressed permission.

She panicked and struggled to close the door tight against the force of fear, trepidation and sheer darkness. The being on the other side appeared much stronger and powerful than she was. If that wasn't enough, she feared what she might witness.

She opened her mouth, attempting to scream for help. But the sound never left her mouth. Only her mind yelled as sheer fear tore 100 MPH through her mind. She tried to pray. Again, all she could do was pray within her heart. "Jesus! Jesus!"

Her heartbeat galloped alongside the blood pounding against her eardrums. Even if she could scream loud enough, she couldn't be absolutely sure her neighbors would hear. Or respond in time. If something bad happened, who'd save her life? She pushed against the door.

As minutes passed, Meredith sensed the visitor was not a kind guest. Not someone lost, needing to use the phone. Rather, an intruder already worked inside her mind, quickly invading her personal space. She wanted him out. Now!

Terror about what was happening consumed her. Why was this nightmare happening to her? Where did the intruder come from? How could she protect herself at the moment?

She couldn't understand how life went from happiness and joy within a few short minutes to chaos, hostility and utter fear.

Just hours ago, she was weary and overwhelmed with house chores—unafraid and seemingly in a great space. all of a sudden, she is fighting for her space not to become invaded. The last thing on her mind, far from what she expected for the evening.

Her thoughts drifted to countless scary movies on television and at movie taverns. Visions of immeasurable variations of fear on the big screen flicker in slow motion. But until that moment, she never witnessed actual terror invade her personal space—nothing she deemed as the possibility of a fight for her life.

All sense of calmness gone, she pushed harder against the door, terrified!

As out of sorts as the moment felt, she could not wrap her mind around the terrorizing grip of insurmountable fear that latched itself onto her. It refused to let go. The intruder wanted into her home, her life at any cost.

Not fighting for her safety and sanity alone—possibly for her life. She must remain alert if she stood any chance of survival until help arrived. That might be hours.

Her cellphone in the other room, all Meredith could do was pray and believe God would protect her from the relentless intruder.

As the unwanted guest pushed harder, she suddenly heard his loud, demanding voice. "Open up and let me in now! I know you're in there. Let me in!" Angry demands laced the coarse, demonic tone.

Scared out of her wits, Meredith fought back with everything. She shouted, "No, no! Go away or I will call the police! I mean it, go away."

She didn't know what to do. If she moved from the door, he'd bust through it.

Opening her mouth wide again, she tried screaming for help but to no avail. Meredith closed her eyes, realizing the unwanted guest was gaining ground upon entry into her home with continuous pushing and kicking at the door.

With nothing else to do, she simply prayed, "Jesus, please help me!"

Suddenly, the fight ceased. The noise stopped. Heavy breathing came through the doorway's crack. Without warning, the door slammed. The lock clicked.

Meredith jumped.

Outside, the previous noise silenced. Left in its place, the wind whispered while crickets chirped in the distance.

She closed her eyes, gasping for breath and silently prayed again. "Jesus, please help me."

To her surprise, she found herself suddenly entertaining quietness both inside her house and outside. Where did this unwanted guest go so quickly? Was he still outside? Waiting for an opportunity to take full advantage of her weakness and force himself into her home?

The music. What happened to the music? Certain she left the music playing before answering the door, why couldn't she still hear it in the background?

Immersed in sweat from head to toe, she went weak in the knees. Shaking and fear stricken, Meredith once again found her voice, only to yell, "Hello, are you still there? What do you want from me? Tell me, what you want from me!"

All of a sudden, Meredith caught a deafening, familiar sound she had heard numerous times. Only this time, it appeared so far away and out of reach.

She strained to make sense of the unidentifiable noise when she abruptly sat up in her bed.

A nightmare. A horrid nightmare. She closed her eyes as breath escaped in a long stream.

The nightmare, so traumatic Meredith almost could not believe it wasn't real. Surreal in the wee hours, Meredith remembered all the dream at once. Thinking about the door...

What about the door?

She bounded from her bed, making a mad dash to the

front door. Everything, including her front door, was indeed intact. Not one thing out of the ordinary. In fact, it was just as she left everything before she went to bed at midnight.

Meredith said to herself, "So what's really happening?"

Was she losing her mind? Was she dreaming, or was some facet of this real with her simply blocking it out?

Eventually, Meredith drifted off and slept into midday. She didn't realize how exhausted the previous night left her. When she finally got up, she was still experiencing, on some level, a sense of sheer overwhelming disbelief.

She could not shake the fear.

She told herself it was just a mistake gone bad, not one she'd make in real life. That particular nightmare was behind her now, and she would continue to focus on her real guests coming to visit. Unbeknownst to them, they would help take her mind off things—especially this terrifying thing.

Less than 48 hours away from Meredith's guests arriving, she was noticeably experiencing a sense of fear, anxiety and dread. Any little noise scared her, making her question the surroundings—even in the privacy and safety of her home.

"Snap out of it already, Meredith. There was nothing to it. Just a silly little mistake in a dream. That's all," she assured herself.

Not being able to shake the overwhelming horror of it all, Meredith decided to visit a counselor via her company's insurance and recommendation. She informed the receptionist it was an emergency. She needed to see someone right away.

At the request of the counselor, Meredith was advised to face her fears by recounting the dream to its fullest details. Advised to simply get the details of the dream as clear as possible, with at least some level of acknowledgment, she could move forward with life as usual.

Meredith realized in order to do that, she might need to practice getting her head back inside the dream, visualizing herself in the scene, gathering all the information she could, and facing her fears head on. Even if she felt it was too much to handle in the moment.

After agreeing to a session with the counselor, Meredith was asked, "Can you identify the intruder? Are there any clues you may have blocked out that lead up to the particular moment of the doorbell ringing and banging on the door?"

The counselor paused, then asked, "Does the day or date when the event took place hold any significance? Why it is taking place? And the number one question—why do you think you were the one chosen for this moment?"

The counselor continued to ask essential questions of Meredith concerning her alleged intruder. "What do you believe to be threatening to invade your space? Do you believe that it could have been a literal intruder, or just your state of mind at the time? Prior to this moment, had you been focusing upon something traumatic, bad news or regretfully expecting a negative outcome about a decision you have to make?"

Another slight pause. "Were you in a bad or an abusive relationship with someone that perhaps seeks revenge? He or she may feel you treated them unfairly or somehow, you may owe them?"

As the session continued, the counselor repeatedly referred to her dream as the dream intruder and theorized that her intruder per se could be a disease trying to break into her spiritual body, trying to steal her peace, confidence and security of her identity.

Before she went out and purchased some elaborate and expensive alarm system, he wanted to make sure she was willing to place all her fears and doubts on the table to be dealt with accurately.

The session continued. What if the dream she had was all in her mind? Maybe about a situation too painful to remember, perhaps she was simply trying hard to block it out.

Seemingly unable to move forward, the counselor suggested that Meredith's ordeal could be a messenger or an ally that she had been in some unresolved relationship. Could it be, the other person felt as though the matter between them still had not been completely resolved?

Honestly, it could have been a million reasons why this happened to Meredith. At that point, the counselor stated they would have to continue talking things out until the matter was properly resolved.

During one of Meredith's visits, she was asked about her spirituality. Did she consider herself a Christian? The counselor wondered aloud whether this issue could have resulted from an earlier childhood incident that somehow had never been addressed or suppressed.

This could be the result of that issue now wanting to bring closure or some sort of healing into her life—perhaps even a power of healing Meredith had not been willing to make room for months or years ago. It could have laid dormant in her life for a long time.

The counselor continued by concluding to Meredith that as with any dream that presents a challenge in our lives, we should find the courage to reenter a dream of the unwanted visitor or intruder. Discover who that intruder represents and then determine what she needed to do in order to move on.

By the end of the first session, Meredith looked thoughtful but didn't confirm nor deny that she was ready to move forward because of the intensity of the dream itself. She ended the session unsure.

"Come, all you who are thirsty, come to the waters;
and you who have no money, come, buy and eat!
Come, buy wine and milk without money and without
cost."

~Isaiah 55:1 (NIV)

Divine Invitation

Returning home from the counselor's office, Meredith had lots on her mind. Her head reeled from all the information she received from the doctor's office concerning the last couple of days since the crazy and out-of-sorts incident happened on her front porch. It still felt so real, as if it happened instead of nothing more than a dream.

The truth of the matter, she found herself stressed more than ever. She couldn't sleep more than four hours a night. She was paranoid everywhere she went by herself, convinced someone was watching or following her at all times.

She wandered in a daze, trying to recall how her life could change so drastically within a few short days.

She wondered aloud, "Is my mind playing tricks on me? Could any of this remotely be true?"

As if life wasn't barreling down on Meredith enough, she eventually noticed quite a few missed calls with messages left on her voicemail.

Dreading to retrieve the voicemail messages, she reluctantly played them back. To her dismay, the call came from her friends, informing her they would have to postpone their planned visit until another time. They ran into some unforeseen difficulties upon planning the trip and could not overlook or change the circumstances.

Therefore, they apologized profusely, voicing their disappointment. They would have to plan their girls' week another time, hoping she would understand and call when she had a moment to catch her breath.

Meredith could definitely understand their plight and quickly agreed another time would be wonderful. Deep down, she desperately wanted to see them now more than ever. She was feeling very unnerved since her encounter with the mysterious, uninvited guest.

Fearing for her safety, admittedly sometimes her life, Meredith questioned if she should pack up and leave the very safe location she lovingly called home for over 10 years. Maybe move to a gated, more expensive location for enhanced protection—even if she had to work a second job to afford it.

Over the next months, Meredith's life never quite returned to what she identified earlier as "normal."

Prior to her previous encounter with the intruder, she was always considered as being upbeat, outgoing, motivated, positive and eager by her family, friends and co-workers. Since her dream, which left her second guessing every move, Meredith could not be absolutely sure if it was in fact a dream or the truth she simply blocked out of her mind. People started noticing the woman they once thought they knew changing right before their eyes.

She found herself constantly nervous, second-guessing her judgment, afraid to be alone, especially at night, and experiencing anxiety at its highest level.

The very thought of being alone, even during the day,

frightened her. She never felt unsafe being out by herself before the incident.

Over the months and years, Meredith saw some disturbing effects from the aftermath of her experience with the intruder being played out in her behavior and communications with others. At times, she could be very curt, short tempered and in some cases, extremely angry in her responses and feedback to others.

Meredith wanted to remain open-minded when dealing with others regardless of who they were. As time passed, she didn't really trust anyone she didn't know well—and some of the ones she did. Inside, she hated herself for feeling that way but couldn't seem to help it.

Within a year or so, she was no longer confident to go out shopping or to dinner alone. She continued feeling as though someone was, in fact, watching her every move.

She also did not find sharing her feelings with co-workers very comfortable. Surely, they wouldn't think too highly of her illusions, so she kept things to herself a lot.

Meredith hated herself for allowing outside forces to change her entire outlook on life. Here she was, at one point in her life used to being energetic, alive, bubbly, outgoing and trusting. The incident made her almost the polar opposite.

She remembered a time when she used to be very outgoing, open and warm. No more. The thought of a stranger coming up and greeting her without proper warning was dismissed quickly.

They wondered, "What happened? Did I do something wrong?"

To which Meredith quickly responded, "Stop, don't

come any closer!'"

Meredith was just trying to make sense of what happened to her "normal" life from a few short years ago. In an interrupted instance, her entire world changed, and she couldn't seem to get it back, no matter how much she tried.

After Meredith apparently tried everything (in her words) to get her life back on the normal track, she still struggled to make even the slightest improvement.

One day, seemingly out of the blue, a co-worker, Sharon, offered Meredith the opportunity to join her for a weekly lunch-time Bible study group.

"Come on," the friend said. "You'll love all the interactions, and all you have to do is to be willing to listen and chime in at your discretion if you'd like to."

Meredith thought to herself, "She must be kidding. This would be the last thing I want to do. Be in the presence of a bunch of total strangers? Not even remotely telling my horrid story. No way."

Later that day, Meredith would never admit this out loud, but she thought quietly within herself, "Maybe, just maybe, one day I could give it a try—even if it meant sitting in the back of the room observing."

At first, Meredith thought attending a Bible study class sounded so intimidating to her. She had never read the Bible or attended a class. In fact, she always thought that because she wouldn't consider herself "perfect," as she liked to say, she wouldn't stand a chance. She never considered herself one that easily fit into that sort of group get-together, so she respectfully declined.

Over the next months, Sharon threw out subtle hints here and there, trying to encourage Meredith to attend. She even went so far as to share how concerned she was about Meredith, but it didn't convince her about the study.

Meredith simply lived her life, fading into the background of everyday existence. Other than her workload, she was out of touch with everything else. After all, she was concentrating on one day living in the Jet Setter Lifestyle. Keep her eye on the dream. That didn't change, and pursuing it didn't require anything outside working hard every day. Pour herself into nice, safe work that kept her from wanting to go out or be around other people much.

She merely existed through life, totally oblivious of its beauty and gracefulness with all God's splendor. Instead of taking one day at a time, Meredith couldn't remember most details of her days, let alone enjoy them.

When asked, "How are you?" her typical response was always, "Oh, I am great! Just taking it one day at a time."

Then rushing off to put out the next makeshift fire, she did anything to avoid other human contact.

Over the next several months, Meredith realized she could barely keep up with her boxed-in routine schedule for long. She was barely eating, sleeping and communicating with others outside daily job responsibilities.

Then one day, during lunchtime, Meredith was once again approached by Sharon. She smiled and reminded her about Bible study the next day at 12:00 noon.

"I'd still love for you to attend with me, and I would even be willing to drive."

Meredith smiled politely. "Thanks. I will give it some thought overnight and let you know first thing in the morning. Okay?"

No idea why Sharon continued to ask her to a class

where she surely would feel most uncomfortable. Wasn't she listening to her at all?

> *"And if it seem evil unto you to serve the Lord, choose you this day whom ye will serve; whether the gods which your fathers served that were on the other side of the flood, or the gods of the Amorites, in whose land ye dwell: but as for me and my house, we will serve the Lord."*
> ~Joshua 24:15 KJV

Open House Now Showing Between Life & Death

Once again, Meredith did not get a good night's sleep, tossing and turning wildly while reminiscing about the horrid nightmare. She found herself thinking more and more about the Bible study class she had been invited to. Was it a good idea for her to attend?

Even though she was nervous and didn't consider herself a Christian, certainly not close to God by any stretch of the imagination, she wondered. Why would God desire to help her at all? Prior to a year ago, she never really talked to Him nor considered herself to have had any interaction with God. And beyond that desperate utterance for help, which she wasn't sure actually happened, she didn't reach out to him after the incident.

Nevertheless, Meredith knew she could not continue her life the same way, tortured both day and night. She was losing it, tired of the empty feelings and space she found herself in.

She was beginning to lose her closest friends from years past. Now, her immediate family members struggled to be there for her because she no longer felt comfortable letting anyone else into her private vortex.

She didn't blame anyone, because honestly, she did not understand it herself. At that point, she felt her life was hopeless and completely over. She dreaded every moment, whether she was asleep or awake.

By the morning, she had made up her mind to attend the Bible class. Not quite convinced why, something deep within encouraged her to go. She couldn't shake the feeling and didn't have a conscious clue about where it came from.

Around 11:00 a.m., Meredith sent Sharon an email to let her know she decided to attend the study. Ecstatic, she informed Meredith to get ready for a shift in her life. She assured her that going forward from today, her life would not be the same.

Not fully understanding exactly what that meant, Meredith took a deep breath and said, "Oh brother, here we go again."

After arriving at the Bible study, Sharon was excited to introduce Meredith as her guest. With cheers and hand claps, she was welcomed by all.

Meredith was taken aback at the warmest welcome she ever received. She could not help but smile and feel embarrassed at the same time. She thought, "Wow, all this for me?"

After a brief introduction from the class members, the group was invited to a lite lunch prepared for the meeting. Meredith was super impressed, growing more relaxed as the meeting progressed.

Soon, the leader of the group opened. "Who has a testimony about how good God has been to them this week?"

Meredith thought, "What? A testimony?" What did that

mean? She thought of a trial where people gave testimonies. But what did that have to do with a Bible study?

Within an instance, one of the other individuals raised his hand and immediately leapt to his feet. He shared that he felt estranged from God for a period of his life, but over the past couple of weeks, he'd been reading more than normal. Praying and reading other books pertaining to the Bible, he sensed the presence of God more and more in his life.

There were more testimonies from the group that caught Meredith's attention, although she did not grasp everything. At least she was paying attention and remained focus while attending the group.

She thought, "Wow, this is interesting."

A few moments later, the group leader announced, "Well, let's all grab our Bibles and get into today's scripture reading, which is coming from Joshua 24:15. Someone read that for me, please."

A clear voice rang out. "And if it seem evil unto you to serve the Lord, choose you this day whom ye will serve; whether the gods which your fathers served that were on the other side of the flood, or the gods of the Amorites, in whose land ye dwell: but as for me and my house, we will serve the Lord." (Joshua 24:15 KJV)

The leader of the Bible study group then asked for open feedback from the attendees. There was quite a bit of various and personal input by those who volunteered to speak.

Then the leader said of Joshua 24:15-28, "It is essential that the service of God's people be performed with a willing mind. For LOVE is the only genuine principle where all acceptable services of God can be received."

He ventured deeper. "The Father seeks only such to

worship him as worship him in spirit and in truth. The carnal mind of man is enmity against God. Therefore, that type of mind is not capable of such spiritual worship."

Suddenly, Meredith was pulled in somehow. Although she considered herself a newbie and definitely unlearned in the group, she was humbly intrigued and wanted to hear more.

She leaned in closer.

Then the leader asked if anyone else had comments?

Another person from the group chimed in. "Though Joshua was clearly put in charge of the group, he did not leave it up to chance or try to make the people choose one concept over the other. He merely allowed them to make their own preference for themselves."

The leader continued. "You see, guys, it is very important that each of us not simply go through life clueless of who we are serving. We must consciously choose for ourselves whether we are serving God as Lord over our lives or the devil? The choice is ours."

At that point, Meredith could not sit back any longer, and before she knew it, she raised her hand. "Um... Excuse me. What are you talking about that we have a choice in the matter? I mean, I am not a believer in God, but I certainly don't believe I am serving the devil. I'm not evil by any means." She shrugged. "I guess I never really thought about it ever being a choice on my part."

The leader said, "Oh yes. Although Jesus died on the cross for each of us at Calvary, John 3:16 is very clear about what we have to do to be born again and make Jesus Christ our Lord and Savior. Someone please turn and read that scripture if you don't mind."

One of the group members flipped through her Bible and read, "For God so loved the world that he gave his one and only Son, that whoever believes in him shall not perish but have eternal life." (John 3:16 NIV)

"Choose whom you will serve, now the matter is laid plainly before you," the leader continued. "Those bound for heaven must be willing to swim against the stream. They must not act as most people do, but as the best do."

He took a sip of water and then continued. "The Israelites agreed with Joshua, being influenced by the example of a man who had been so great a blessing to them. 'We also will serve the Lord,' they responded.

"See how much good great men do, by their influence, if zealous in religion?

"Joshua brought them to express the full purpose of heart to cleave to the Lord—meaning they stuck to him like a fly on honey. They had to abandon their sense of all self-confidence in their own sufficiency. Else their purposes would be in vain.

"Instead, they deliberately chose the service of God, and Joshua bound them to it by a solemn covenant. As a reminder, he set up a monument. In this affecting manner, Joshua took his last leave of them. If they perished, their blood would be upon their own heads."

The participants sat for a moment, contemplating as the class came to a close. Like the end of every meeting, the question was asked. "Is there anyone in attendance that would like to accept Jesus Christ into their lives today? If so, bow your heads, close your eyes and repeat this prayer."

The leader paused for a few seconds, waiting. "According to Romans 10:9-10, if you declare with your mouth, 'Jesus is Lord,' and believe in your heart that God raised him from the dead, you will be saved. For it is with your heart that you believe and are justified, and it is with your mouth that you profess your faith and are saved."

With that, the class was dismissed until the following Wednesday. Everyone once again greeted one another and rushed back to their respective jobs.

On the way back to work, Sharon was beaming, overjoyed that Meredith decided to attend the study. "I hope you'll agree to come again next week. No pressure!"

Meredith was still in shock, intrigued and eager to learn more about God. How could someone like herself possibly draw close to Him? She wanted to know, especially since her encounter with the darkness left her frightened for her life. As they drove toward the office, Meredith inquired about this Bible study. Was it always this intense?

The following week, Meredith could not wait for Sharon to ask whether she would like to go. Instead, she called and offered to drive this time around. Unable to explain the deep desire, Meredith only knew for the first time in a long time, she felt some relief after her traumatic ordeal.

The weekly Bible study group continued on the previous week's topic of choosing whom you will serve. Meredith was very pleased, because she especially wanted to know more about this choosing process.

The leader said, "As a recap from last week, Joshua encouraged the people to express full purpose of heart and to cleave to the Lord. They had to come away from all confidence in their own sufficiency, else their purposes would be in vain. As they made service of God their deliberate choice, Joshua bound them to it by a solemn covenant."

His eyes searched the group's faces. "Do you understand what I am saying?"

The group responded with an resounding yes.

A few uttered, "God is good."

The instructor continued. "For next week, class, I want to challenge each of you to revisit the lesson we just covered. Provide some thoughts about how you can entrust matters that are important to you into the hands of God so that you won't have to carry the load alone."

Another momentary pause, letting his words sink in. "The Israelites responded as Joshua finished. 'Though the house of God, the Lord's table, and even the walls and trees before which we have uttered our solemn purposes of serving him, would bear witness against us if we deny him, yet we may trust in him, that he will put his fear into our hearts, that we shall not depart from him.' God alone can give grace, yet he blesses our endeavors to engage men to his service."

That day, just as Sharon promised, something truly shifted in Meredith's thinking. She experienced a greater sense of ease and assurance that everything was going to be alright. She wasn't sure how, but by the same token, she believed it would. She was glad she took Sharon's advice.

Driving back to work, Meredith was beaming both inside and out. Speechless, the only emotion she could display was tears of joy and gladness.

Experienced from her personal walk with Christ, Sharon understood. "No explanation needed. I get it."

They rode back to work in total silence.

Photo Credit 1 MonikaP_https://cdn.pixabay.com/photo/2016/07/07/22/43/rise-1503338_960_720.jpg

Knock, Knock-Who's There?

Months into the weekly Bible study group, Meredith was gaining her confidence back and feeling better than ever. A new born-again believer, she was growing in Christ daily. In fact, she was even sleeping better at night and loving every minute of her new posture in the Word of God.

The news was so good, she could not wait to tell everyone she knew and ran into about her weekly sessions at the local Bible study. Of course, some thought she totally lost it, and then there were those who simply did not want to hear anything she had to say relating to the Bible.

Some remarked, "No thanks, I already know enough about Him. I'm good."

While responses were at times rude, mean-spirited and outlandish, Meredith was glad she found a new outlook on her recent stressful turn of events. At that point, she vowed to continue learning more about Jesus and her personal walk in relationship with Him.

Weeks, months—another year went by after Meredith began her personal journey walking with God. She was more assured, eager and excited to grow in Him. It felt like she could take on anything put in her way and walk away with the victory in tow.

One night, after taking her shower and preparing for bed, happy as a lark and confident as ever, Meredith got into bed. With her favorite praise and worship CDs playing, before long, she was off to a sweet sleep in the Lord. At first, her rest was peaceful, and she was smiling even in her dreams.

Suddenly, a presence loomed over Meredith, and it wasn't a peaceful feeling at all. In fact, the presence felt familiar, as though she experienced it before. Attempting to wake herself up, she was unable to move to either side. Neither could she open her eyes.

To Meredith's surprise, instantly the nightmare from years earlier came back with a vengeance, haunting her. It tried to strip away her newfound joy, peace and happiness. She remembered the episode at the doorway. The rapid knocking and excessive ringing of the doorbell. No! Not again!

Meredith fought to catch her breath and stay sober minded. Her thoughts raced. She was losing consciousness as the horrific panic settled in. The knocks in her dreams grew louder.

Once again, the demonic voice of the intruder screamed, "Let me in. Let me in!"

At that moment, when Meredith didn't think she had enough strength to continue the fight, she remembered the name of Jesus. She cried out in her weakness. "Jesus, Jesus, please help me. Save me, sweet Jesus!"

Everything stopped.

When she woke up later, Meredith found herself safe and sound, still in bed with the beautiful sunshine coming through her window. As she moved about freely in her bed, she realized she was no longer under the bondage of attack by the enemy.

Looking around her bedroom, she observed that her

room suddenly reflected calmness and comfort that she was being divinely protected. The same calm she experienced prior to going to sleep just hours earlier.

After taking it all in, she drew in a deep breath and said quietly, "Thank you, sweet Jesus. In Your Name, You did it again!"

Still learning and growing in God, she had not fully grasped all the benefits that came with the Name of Jesus, but she was catching on quickly.

That week, when Meredith attended the Bible study, she decided to share her heart about the demonic dream with the class. By then, she felt as though she was studying with others whom she considered her friends. Friends who looked out for each other in prayer.

She wanted them to know she was hounded and haunted by these reoccurring nightmares. She wanted desperately for them to stop, but no longer wanted to fight the battle alone. She needed reinforcement to step in—to assist her.

She believed God was with her, but she also solicited some earthly foot patrol as well. Not fully understanding how prayer in itself worked, she knew enough to simply choose to believe in the Name of Jesus.

"I know, I know!" shouted a brother from the class. "I believe we should stand on the scripture reference coming from Proverbs 3:7. The NIV reads, 'Do not be wise in your own eyes; fear the LORD and shun evil.'"

"What exactly does that mean?" asked Meredith. "Can someone elaborate on that a little more for me, please?"

The leader piped up. "Sure. In Proverbs 3:7-8, we are advised not to become wise in our own eyes. In other words, we should not become puffed up with a vain conceit of our own wisdom. As if our understanding has enough sufficiency for the conduct of all our affairs."

He searched Meredith's face for understanding, then continued. "Without direction and assistance from God, we are automatically doomed from the start. As believers in God, we are admonished to fear the Lord, to reverence God's wisdom, and despise our own guess work at best."

Meredith nodded.

"Why?" the leader asked. "Because in doing so, it shall be health to your body, which is signified by one important part of it. And marrow to the bones — which is the nourishment and strength of the bones—and a great preserver and prolonger of life."

Someone else chimed in at that point. "This fear of God, or true religion, is not only necessary to the salvation of the soul, but is also calculated to promote the health of the body. Through trusting God, it prevents and protects us from making erroneous mistakes or fearing the enemy."

Meredith nodded again. It made sense. She drank in the remainder of the study time.

Once again, she left the class feeling positive and confident that with God, all things were going to be possible for her life—including dealing with this demonic intruder, determined to challenge her relentlessly until she surrender her will for his.

Meredith was learning she didn't have to bow down to the pressures of this enemy. Instead, she needed to trust God for her safety and to cast all of her cares, fears and doubts upon Him. He alone would take care of and protect her.

She smiled to herself all the way back to work. Each time she attended the weekly Bible study, she walked away with a nugget of some sort to help her along the way.

She thought out loud, "Wow, where have I been that I was missing out on a life-changing ordeal?"

*"By their fruit **you will** recognize **them**. Do people pick grapes from thorn bushes, or figs from thistles?"*
~Matthew 7:16 (NIV)

Always Ask for General Identification

As time passed, Meredith found herself in a good place financially, mentally and spiritually. In fact, she actually considered dating since she had worked hard and experienced success on a level she hoped for. The one thing she found missing from her life was a wonderful spouse to share her success.

She didn't care much for dating sites or apps and avoided them at all costs. However, she was opened to meeting people the old-fashioned way through time and chance, or through introductions primarily by family and friends. She even joined the singles group at the church. No pressure, of course.

Approximately six months after connecting with the single's ministry, Meredith met George. According to Meredith standards, George appeared to be a handsome, smart, intelligent man with a love for the Word of God as well.

She had no reason to doubt that. After all, he was in church every Sunday and part of several ministries. He appeared to be a genuine and honest human being.

The other thing that caught Meredith's attention was that George appeared to be so loving and attentive to the needs of ALL the other ladies in the church. Walking them to their cars, pulling out chairs at the table. Opening doors—just an all-around gentleman.

After any singles event in or outside the church, he made sure all the ladies arrived at their cars safely. In some cases, he asked them to call him once they arrived safely. He wanted to make sure they were home and inside without incident.

Heck, George even made sure all the ladies' needs were met every week and some days in between, insisting he kept an updated roster. He monitored their phone numbers, email, Facebook accounts, Snapchat and even the mailing address of each single lady in the ministry.

That George was a bad boy. Rather, George was a well-rounded Christian man with good old-fashioned morals and respect for all the ladies within the single ministry. Truly a brother to all—in the Lord of course.

Meredith, bless her heart, thought this was just so sweet and loving of George, and she marveled within herself.

To find a man like George for a husband would be wonderful. Good ole George. What a catch he would make for some lucky woman.

As various outings continued, Meredith notice all the women in the group had nothing but nice, godly things to say about George's character.

"George is a blessed man."

"George is so well-rounded and versed in the Word of God."

"George is willing to help any of the ladies out at the drop of a hat. You can depend upon George, yes indeed."

Yep, time and again, good ole George always delivered. He always kept his promises, desires, hopes, and the hopes of others, close to his vest. He was a sharp dresser too, a smooth operator and a hit around the ladies. His swag was something to be modeled by other men.

From the words of George's lips himself, he always ended his classes with a phrase. *"You can always depend upon George to be there for any of you ladies. Yes sir, there's no job too big or too small. Day or night, call me, and I'll be there for you."*

The women were delighted they had such an incredibly supportive member amongst their small group. Repeatedly, George held true to his promises, dedicated all the way.

Over the years, the single ministry group grew larger and larger, and the ladies saw less and less of George.

One weekend, Meredith decided to go shopping and treat herself to a nice, leisurely lunch. After ordering, she heard a familiar voice behind her. As she stopped to take notice, well, what do you know? It was good ole George. Smiling so hard you could see all 32 pearly whites two blocks away!

Meredith thought to herself, "Wow. Seeing George up close and personal, his teeth are so white it must look like the entry into the pearly gates themselves. If he gets any closer, I might have to break out my shades just to remain focused."

Rushing to the table to greet her, George said, "Well, hello there beautiful. You're looking as delicious as a Georgia peach. How are you, and how have you been?"

Meredith, glad to see him as well, smiled back and even gave George a warm hug. "I'm fine—just been keeping myself busy, that's all. How about yourself?"

"Oh, you know, been keeping myself busy with various projects here and there. Trying to stay faithful unto the Lord.

Yep, you know that I woke up early with my mind like they say. Stayed on Jesus!"

"We've missed you, George. Where have you been?"

"Well, I've been missing the class because of my busy work schedule, and I haven't been able to see all the ladies lately. I been wondering how everyone is doing."

Meredith quickly filled in the gap for him and inquired whether he had lunch yet.

George, picking up on what he thought was a queue, immediately responded. "No, and I would love to join you. I mean, if that's what you are asking. The last thing I would want to do is self-impose myself upon your free time alone."

Meredith, still smiling, obliged him and said, "Why, yes, that would be lovely. Please have a seat."

While enjoying lunch together, they both chatted about their lives and their eventual hopes and desires. Meredith confided in George that one day she would love to get married and settle down.

George took everything, intense interest on his face— almost as if mentally recording it all.

"Yes, I know what you mean my sister. I am very much interested in getting married myself someday and settling down with a fine, fine lovely woman who has her act together. One that is loving and just loves the Lord and all."

After lunch, like always, George walked Meredith to her car, making small talk. He eventually got around to asking her out later in the week for a date to the movies and possibly dinner afterward.

"No strings attached of course," he assured her. "It will be just a friendly dinner and two mature singles out having fun. You can trust me, remember. I am reliable, fun, dependable, and of course, a godly man who respects all women—both in and out of the church. No sir, I know how to remain respectable at all times." He flashed his big smile at her.

"By the way, we should exchange personal phone numbers. Just in case something comes up and neither of us can make it. You know, just as a precautionary measure, right?"

Excitement pulsed through Meredith. Imagine that. She had an opportunity for an innocent date with George. No strings attached. Elated at having George's full attention, she would be able to see a different perspective of him.

She eagerly provided George with her personal cell-phone number. "Here. Please feel free to call me anytime."

They parted, Meredith praying he'd use it.

Part Three

"Be anxious for nothing, but in everything by prayer and supplication with thanksgiving let your requests be made known to God."
~Philippians 4:6 (NASB)

I Just Assumed It was You Lord

Over the next several months, Meredith enjoyed her time with George. Occasionally, they went out to the movies, dinner, football games, and of course, they attended singles' events together.

George wanted more from the relationship than Meredith was willing to provide or allow herself to have.

He had been searching for a woman like Meredith that he could spend the rest of his life with, eventually getting married, traveling the world. Someday they'd start a family when the time was right and become the world greatest parents. George realized from just one look at Meredith that day, he was hooked. His heart was smitten for her.

Now realizing that that chance for them might not ever happen, he was heartbroken and dismayed. Even though he and Meredith often stayed in touch by phone—a lot—that wasn't enough, George wanted more, much more.

Still, both Meredith and George swore it was just two good friends, enjoying each other's company. That's absolutely all. No strings attached. Right? Little did Meredith realize, silently, George was growing tired of the pretense.

As the months passed, George was beginning to see their time spent together as something better as husband and wife rather than as a simple "friendship" or being really good friends.

If the truth be told, Meredith really felt the same way. But she was terrified about taking that next step which would be huge for her and she was afraid of failing or that George might not completely feel the exact same way about her. She was just not willing to take that chance and be let down.

For that reason, Meredith always made sure she kept things above board. She didn't notice any red flags, although they were planted right before her eyes.

Although she enjoyed George's company, she pretended that she too didn't want more from the relationship, friendship or whatever she chose to call the thing with George.

She figured if she keep telling herself that if she wasn't interested in him from a serious romantic perspective, it would make sense. Bottom line, she was afraid to fall head over hills in love. Telling herself that she was not involved in an "eventually let's get married" type of relationship, she would not allow herself to go any further.

If she even sensed the conversation of a much serious relationship might come up, she would beat George to the punch by saying to him, "I'm not ready to get married." During their time together, Meredith knew exactly want she wanted in a husband—and what she did not.

In the meantime, Meredith continued regularly attending her weekly Bible study class and was enthused about her upward growth in the Word of God.

She eagerly shared her class sessions with George— things she was learning and excited about from her weekly classes. It didn't take Meredith very long before noticing that George was becoming wary of the dialogue with him being "always about church."

Meredith explained that she saw her attendance at the study as less about church and more about building a personal awareness of her divine connection with a God who loves and desires the very best for her.

"Today's lesson was about being anxious for nothing." She asked George, "Do you know that particular scripture?"

Unimpressed, George answered, "Yes, I know it well. It's not my favorite, but I am aware of it.

Meredith continued, "At first, I must admit I didn't quite get its meaning. However, when the leader explained more in-depth, my spiritual eyes were opened to its bigger picture."

Suddenly, George took in a deep breath and held it as long as he could before it let it out. Seeming interested, he let out a great big Georgia smile that looked less than sincere.

That didn't stop Meredith. "You see George, I learned that God knows what and who is best for me to share my life with. If I only trust and rely upon Him, in due time, I will reap the perfect harvest for me. Do you agree with that, George?" He didn't respond. "George, do you agree with that statement?"

Preoccupied by his watch, he looked eager to change the subject. He seemed a bit unnerved by the conversation.

Then he chimed in. "Oh, what about the part that says, 'but in everything by prayer and supplication, with thanksgiving, let your requests be made known to God?' I mean doesn't that count for something special?"

"Well, yes. But if I'm anxious, which means I'm worried, concerned, restless, fretful and apprehensive about everything, including relationships, I might try to get ahead of God. Then I might make the wrong choice or choices based solely on what something looks like as opposed to what it really is inside."

She searched his face, trying to read his expression. "Do you agree, George? Have you ever thought you were in love or had some special feelings for someone, only to find out that the more time you spent with that person, they really weren't what or who you had in mind? He or she was a wonderful person, but not someone you wanted to spend the rest of your life with."

George fidgeted a bit before looking at his watch. "My, my. Look at the time. Where has it gone?" He stood. "I've got to get back to the office. I forgot I still have lots and lots of things to finish up before the end of the day. If you want to get together this weekend for a bit, just give me a call. Have a blessed day."

Without so much as a hug or wave, he sprinted off.

Feeling a little odd, Meredith did not know what to make of George's sudden change of posture toward her. He wasn't the same ole jovial, over-the-top, bubbly, charming man she was used to seeing—both in the classroom and earlier in the times they spent together.

That wasn't all she realized about George's attitude and posture toward her. Within the next couple days, Meredith noticed he was hard to get in touch with. She tried making several calls to his cell phone only to be forced to leave a message and wait for him to contact her.

She even at some point tried calling his work phone. Still no response from George. Meredith started to worry.

"What if something terrible happened to George after all? No one else had heard from George either. Not even the singles' minister.

When Meredith finally made contact with George, she was rather shocked by his new demeanor. He appeared distant, distracted—and a little on the defensive side.

Even basic questions appeared too much for George to answer.

"George, where have you been? I've missed seeing you around. Are you okay?"

"Oh, really? The last time we spoke, you acted as though it really didn't matter if we saw each other again."

Meredith was shocked, taken aback by his coldness. Catching her breath, she finally asked, "Did I do or say something inappropriate to warrant this response?"

"Oh no. I was just joking with you. Having a little fun. I am doing well. Just been a little busy that's all. How about things with you?"

From that day forward, Meredith gave much consideration and thought to the lessons she learned during her Bible study sessions. It seemed that whatever lessons they studied in class, she could readily use that knowledge. Sometimes, within the next couple of days.

Not only was she thankful for the wisdom, but it caused her to pay more attention to her spiritual discernment. Something she had never been previously tuned into before. Honestly, until then, Meredith never realized just how much she had not been aware.

Over the next several months, where George was concerned, she found herself praying more and talking less. She wanted to be a genuine friend to George, but she believed his expectations of their "friendship" were more than she was willing to offer him. At least for the time—

especially since his emotions appeared to be all over the place. At any given moment, she really didn't know what to expect from him or what mood he would be in.

During her prayer time, Meredith spent a lot of time before God, asking Him to please show her privately if she was missing something vital concerning her friendship with George.

At times, she was left bewildered from her conversations with George. Still, there were moments she felt drawn to him and his sweetness.

Meredith was willing to take more risks instead of instantly withdrawing and ghosting those she didn't readily feel a connection with—such as the case with George.

She genuinely wanted to help George emotionally and be there for him if he needed a real friend. The more time she spent praying for George, the more she felt compel to see this at times rocky "friendship" through.

She asked God if George could remotely be the one for her, despite how she currently felt about him. As far as she could see, even though he was a nice gentleman, she could not see herself in a marital relationship with him.

Or could she?

"But if we walk in the light, as he is in the light, we have fellowship with one another, and the blood of Jesus, his Son, purifies us from all sin."
~1 John 1:7 (NIV)

Friendship or Followership

Hello everyone. It's good to see each of you today at our noon Bible study. Come on in, grab a plate for lunch, and settle in for an incredible time together. Is everyone excited to be here?" the bible study leader shouted.

A roar from the class rose. "Yes, we are!"

With that, the class began.

"Today's lesson will be coming from the scripture reference of 1 John 1:7. *But if we walk in the light, as he is in the light, we have fellowship with one another, and the blood of Jesus, his Son, purifies us from all sin.*" (NIV)

"This lesson has everything to do with how we communicate with each other and the importance of getting an understanding."

Meredith's ears perked up. Once again, she was intrigued. Each time she attended the class, she always left with a greater perspective. Today's session, she realized, would not disappoint.

The group leader opened. "Poor communication has been the plague of mankind ever since the tower of Babel. The following statements reveal today that we still face problems when trying to communicate to one another."

The group listened quietly, nodding as he rattled off the

statements.

"I know you believe you understand what you think I said, but I'm not sure you realized that what you heard is not what I meant."

The instructor continued. "We can sometimes be misunderstood because of mispronunciations. As when Howard Hendrick's child told a friend that his father taught in a 'cemetery.'"

Most everyone in the group chuckled.

"Sometimes sound-alike phrases are misunderstood, as with the child in a Christian school who was asked to draw a picture depicting the hymn "Gladly the Cross I'd Bear." Instead, the child drew a picture of Gladly, the cross-eyed bear."

Thunderous laughter exploded from everyone in the classroom.

"Not only that," the instructor said, "but we have problems understanding the concept of each other as well. There is nothing compared to the problems we encounter understanding the concepts of God, for His thoughts are not our thoughts, they are foreign to us."

Meredith leaned forward.

"So how do we communicate with God concerning His thoughts toward us?" Intent, none of the group spoke, so he continued. "Now, God has given us His thoughts in the Bible and explained them carefully. But as time passed, they have become Greek to us, and we have warped His thoughts and reverted to our own practices concerning His Word.

"One such concept that has been especially warped in the biblical meaning is the concept of Christian fellowship. Today, churches have fellowship halls, fellowship dinners, and fellowship retreats, but very few are willing to have real authentic fellowship with one another."

He had Meredith's full attention, as if speaking straight to her.

"Yet for a church that seeks to be guided in the principle and practice by the New Testament, fellowship is very vital. This afternoon, I hope each of you will learn that biblical fellowship is God's method for the outworking of His will and through the church.

"In order for you to understand this, we will have to discover first, what true fellowship really means. Second, why fellowship is important in a New Testament church, and finally, how each one of us can practice fellowship here at our weekly Bible study."

He pause only a moment. "At our next meeting, we will look at the biblical meaning of fellowship and what it means to the survival of a church body."

Meredith was literally blown away by the download of information God allowed her to receive within one hour of this class.

It shifted something in her thinking about friendship with George. She couldn't help but wonder if she and George were simply experiencing miscommunication problems when they spoke with each other. She was more convinced that George thought of their friendship as much more than she ever said or imagined. She could tell by the non-verbal and sometimes reluctant way he communicated with her. It was as if he tried everything within his power to avoid her at all costs.

The next week at mid-week Bible study, Meredith was front and center when the instructor began to teach.

"Remember we left off with me explaining the Bible's

Meaning of Fellowship. As we go back into history and dig deep into the original languages of the Bible, we discover seven significant facts that help us understand God's intended meaning of the word 'fellowship.'

"The first fact concerns the meaning of the Greek root.

"Our English word 'fellowship' is the translation of the Greek word 'koinonia.' This Greek word is derived from the root 'koinos,' which was a prefix in ancient Greek.

"Add it to a prefix word meaning 'living,' 'owning a purse,' 'a dispute,' you would get words meaning 'living in community together.' So we see that the root of the word 'fellowship' means 'to hold something in common.'

"Our second fact relates to the usage of the word fellowship.

"Koinonia was used to describe corporations, labor guilds, partners in a law firm, and the most intimate of marriage relationships.

From the usage of the word, we can conclude that fellowship is a word denoting a relationship that is dependent on more than one individual—an interdependent relationship.

"Questions so far anyone?"

Not only were there no questions, but everyone was leaning forward and hanging on every word being taught. To Meredith, it was as if someone had been eavesdropping on her last conversation with George, which had been a while.

The leader continued. "Finally, the third and last fact is that fellowship was never used to describe man's relationship to God before the coming of the Holy Spirit to indwell the church. It is an exclusively post-Pentecostal relationship."

Meredith looked around. She was extremely thankful that God placed her in such an incredible Work/Life/Balance Bible Study class that took place during their lunch hour on the job once a week.

This class opened up a whole new world for her and others to further learn of God's goodness to her. He cared about all the things that concerned her daily walk in Him.

She appreciated more and more that he was mindful of her at all times. It didn't matter if she was awake or sleep. Tired or energized. Frustrated or at total peace. She was beginning to trust God at all times and in all things. For that, she was extremely grateful.

On the way home from work that day, Meredith came to a conclusion, pondering the day's Bible study. Followership is the action of someone who serves in a subordinate role. It could also be considered a specific set of skills that complement leadership or a role within a hierarchical organization.

She considered the meaning of "followership" being "a social construct integral to the leadership process, or the behaviors engaged in while interacting with leaders in an effort to meet organizational objectives or a personal need."

Either way, both descriptions gave her much to contemplate. Meredith had to come to terms that perhaps this was the way she visualized her friendship with George, rather than a person who did not want to rule or control her but instead wanted to love her and be a part of her life.

Unwanted Guest

Over the next several weeks, Meredith noticed that she had not seen nor heard from George in a while. She hadn't seen him at the single's ministry either. She realized George entered her life for a reason but was also curious whether it could possibly be for a season.

She thought about contacting him and perhaps inviting him out to lunch—just as a friend, of course—but did not want to complicate matters worse, especially since their last encounter did not go well.

Weeks turned into months, and eventually, months turned into a year and things were continually improving for Meredith, both financially and personally. She was thinking clearer, and she had a greater perspective on life and how to accomplish her dreams, making them her reality.

The holidays came and went, and Meredith was in such a good space. She found herself not being overly anxious about anything and took more time out for herself than she ever did before. Never had she known greater insight and confidence as she felt since spending quality time in the presence of God.

For the first time in years, she was thoroughly enjoying her life in ways she never imagined, and she was loving every moment of it. Every day, Meredith found herself thanking God at every interval.

She thanked him for all of his manifold blessings. Things

she was painfully aware of and even those things she was clueless about. Being in the presence of God made Meredith more mindful and aware of just how much Jesus really loved her.

From time-to-time, Meredith was just like everyone else. Of course, she dreamed and hoped that she would one day find the love of her life and settle down with a family. She didn't want to move too quickly but wanted to be in God's timing for her life and potential family.

Embarrassed to admit it, she caught herself reminiscing about 18 months earlier when she first met George. He appeared a possible candidate for the two of them together in the future. Of course, she would never remotely suggest such a thing publically, let alone tell him to his face.

Just as quickly as that thought came to Meredith, she remembered thinking that although her first contact with George appeared to be refreshing and enjoyable, she noticed he probably wanted much more. But she didn't see any possibilities of their relationship advancing in that direction. By all intents and purposes, they were not remotely compatible. George was hyper, and she was hypo.

Two months in to the New Year, while out having lunch with some of her co-workers, Meredith noticed a man sitting across the room from theirs. With his back to them, she couldn't help but think, "Is that George having lunch by himself?"

By the time she made her move over toward the table, the man had disappeared.

After a while, Meredith allowed the thought and incident to pass. A couple weeks later, while at the mall shopping alone, on her way out to the car, she looked across the parking lot. A familiar car was parked two cars down from hers, a man sitting at the steering wheel. His head down, a baseball cap covered most of his face.

Strangely, Meredith's eyes were drawn to the car. Once again, she sensed that the man looked familiar. Yes, he could even be George. Not understanding why, she felt compelled to call out his name as she approached her car, and did.

Hurrying forward, as she got closer, she called his name again. "George, is that you?"

With no response, the guy in the car quickly started the engine and backed out, leaving the parking lot. No acknowledgement that he even heard her voice. The man looked straight ahead and left with no fanfare.

Once again, Meredith thought, I am losing it for sure. How in the world could I have thought this stranger was George? Surely it could not have been. I am sure he would have acknowledged me. Right? Why wouldn't he?

On Good Friday that year, Meredith decided to reach out and invite her old friend, George, to lunch. She did miss his company and thought they could use that time for a great meal and to catch up on each other's progress since they last met.

She extended the lunch invitation, and he readily accepted. They agreed to meet at noon on Friday that same week at a familiar restaurant where they ate before. At the restaurant, both George and Meredith greeted each other with big smiles and friendly hugs.

George spoke first. "Look at you—looking good. How have you been?"

"Wow, thanks, George. You look good yourself. I have been keeping myself busy and keeping my focus on things that matter."

"Hmmm. Is that why you invited me to lunch this week, because I matter to you?"

Meredith was careful to answer the question with a lot of thought, not giving George any false hope of anything special between the two of them. She didn't miss him in that manner.

In the meantime, George stared deeply into her eyes, waiting for a response.

Meredith thought to herself, "God, I hope this nice gesture does not turn into a mistake of me asking him out to what I thought was going to be a friendly lunch."

Still determined to make it a wonderful experience of a simple lunch together, Meredith forged ahead, changing the subject without answering his question.

After lunch, George walked Meredith back to her car before saying goodbye. "Can we see each other again?"

Meredith, being unsure, said, "I'll definitely think about it. But I want to make sure you understand. I only like you as a friend and nothing else. Are we clear on that?"

George looked at her straight in the eyes, a slight smile playing with his lips. "Yes, of course. What did you think I meant?"

Meredith didn't want to stir the pot any further. "I just wanted to make sure we were both on the same page, and I didn't want there to be any mixed signals."

On the way out of the parking lot, the thought came to Meredith that it would have been a great time to ask George about the times she thought she saw him at the restaurant and mall. She thought better of it and decided to simply let the moment pass.

"To man belong the plans of the heart, but
from the Lord comes the reply of the tongue.
All a man's ways seem innocent to him, but
motives are weighed by the Lord."
~Proverbs 16:1-2 (BSB)

Strategic Foresight

As Monday morning dawned, Meredith was super-duper excited about the week's Bible study. It had been a while since everyone saw each other and had an opportunity to share all the great things God had done for them. Wanting the company, Meredith texted Sharon and asked if they could ride together on Wednesday.

Counting down the time, Wednesday lunchtime finally arrived, and Meredith and Sharon were on their way to the weekly bible study. As they drove, Meredith turned to Sharon and said, "Sharon, I want to share with you just how much I have grown spiritually since the first day you invited me to the class. You have no idea just how much I have been blessed and have learned."

Likewise, Sharon spoke up and said to Meredith, "I feel the same way about our time spent together there and also our rides to and from the class. I get joy just seeing the smile on your face and the confidence in your daily walk being strengthened."

Meredith tried to put into words her thankfulness for what she realized was a divine blessing. She didn't have the vocabulary to express adequately her gratitude. Thank you felt far too shallow.

After arriving to the parking where they held the Bible study, Meredith turned to Sharon once again. "Honestly, the time spent in the classes has been a blessing to me. I just wanted to thank you for the special invite and for the total acceptance into loving, warm and caring extended family weekly gatherings."

On another note, Meredith felt it necessary to let Sharon in on how God opened her eyes to how she could personally interpret scripture for her own life, confident in making better decisions and judgment calls in every area.

Sharon appeared intrigued and asked Meredith to please elaborate. Meredith shared that prior to attending the first class, she was being haunted by a horrific nightmare that little-by-little robbed her of confidence, security, peace of mind, enjoyment and the everyday desire to do things she once loved.

She continued that once things started improving along those lines, she started to attend a single's bible study class at her local church and although she met some pretty interesting people this one particular person that she met is well versed in the bible, polite, smart, handsome and…

When Meredith stopped talking for a minute, Sharon asked, "Is anything wrong?"

"Oh no. I just find it a little difficult sharing. I don't want to sound negative or as if I am stabbing him in the back."

"I completely understand. You don't have to say anything if you don't want to share."

By then, they had arrived at the Bible study, and once again, after the meet and greet was over and lunch had been served, the class started with prayer and highlights from their last meeting. Next came the testimonials from the group.

As the leader began to prep for the day's lesson, he announced that he had been struggling with the need to specifically intercede for someone in the class for their divine protection.

It had been in his heart for over a month or more to pray and intercede that God would watch over and protect that person from the evil one who desired to sift him or her like wheat.

The leader said he sensed that this individual's life could somehow end up being in grave danger further down the road, and he encouraged the class to join him in prayer that this individual would be divinely protected by God's grace and mercy.

He also encouraged the group to continue in prayer with him for the safety and protection of all those who were in attendance and those who joined in the future.

While his intent was not to place fear in the lives of those in attendance, he wanted to make everyone alert and aware of unforeseen dangers that lurk about in the world.

"Okay," the instructor announced, "let's continue with today's lesson, which we will be reading from Proverbs 16:1-2. 'To man belongs the plans of the heart, but from the Lord comes the reply of the tongue. All a man's ways seem innocent to him, but motives are weighed by the Lord.' (BSB)"

He stopped and let the words simmer for a moment before continuing.

"What is strategic foresight? And how does it work for the Christian leader? Would anyone care to comment in their own words?"

Finally, someone spoke up and ventured, "Having the ability to see an issue or a certain problem before it takes place?"

"Thanks for sharing. Okay, anyone else? Didn't Jesus say, 'Do not worry about tomorrow, for tomorrow will worry about itself? Each day has enough trouble of its own.' (Matt. 6:34 NIV) Are we to plan for the future? Is it like fortune telling or palm reading? Or do we just ask God to bless our prognostications?"

Several blank stares met the leader.

"In other words, are we to spend time among ourselves trying to create our own path in life, or do we depend upon God for guidance and leadership?"

Several murmured their thoughts.

The instructor continued. "According to Richard Slaughter, 'Strategic foresight is the ability to create and maintain a high-quality, coherent and functional forward view and to use the insights arising in organizationally useful ways. It can also represent a fusion of future methods with those of strategic management.' Strategic planning is one of the fundamental skills a leader possesses.

"For the remainder of our class, let's all take a look at Strategic Foresight and Who God Is. God is omniscient, omnipresent and eternal. Therefore, He knows everything about everybody in the past, present and future. So how do we package that in our space-time continuum?"

He paused. No one spoke.

"God has perfect strategic foresight in, over and into our lives," he continued. "He makes absolutely no mistakes at all. God is perfect at all things. This is such a difficult concept for mankind to grasp. We hear it. We read it. We even pray it. Still, at the end of the day, it is very difficult to totally accept.

"God's character is revealed to us as being Creator of all that is powerful, majestic, and sovereign over all creation, loving, compassionate, patient, perfectly righteous, just and holy. God is."

Heads nodded as a smattering of uttered agreement filled the room.

"Combined, these characteristics are the building blocks to perfect strategic foresight. God's purposes encompass the whole range from eternity past to eternity future, and they extend to every part of His dominion.

"He knows the future. Jeremiah 29:11 says, 'For I know the plans I have for you,' declares the Lord, 'plans to prosper you and not to harm you, plans to give you hope and a future.'" (NIV)

More heads nodded, tracking with the leader.

He pushed on. "Next, since we have a little more time left for discussion, let's look also at the Strategic Foresight and Who We Are. God has perfect strategic foresight. We can, at best, achieve imperfect strategic foresight, or, at worst, thoughtless hindsight.

"Notice in Proverbs, Solomon, the wisest man of all times, said, 'To man belong the plans of the heart, but from the Lord comes the reply of the tongue. All a man's ways seem innocent to him, but motives are weighed by the Lord.' (Proverbs 16:1-2 BSB)

"Finally, let's also take a look at the Strategic Foresight and How It Works. According to a famous quote from Peter Drucker, 'The best way to predict the future is to create it.'

Drucker also states that 'Plans are only good intentions unless they immediately degenerate into hard work.' The only thing we know about the future is that it will be different."

The instructor went on to say, "Trying to predict the future is like trying to drive down a country road at night with no lights while looking out the back window."

He waited while everyone had a moment to let the words sink into their brains.

As time grew short, the instructor wrapped up. "For today's lesson, we as born again believers especially do not have to waste our time or spend unnecessary energy, sweat and tears worrying about our tomorrows and future plans. The True and Living God already worked them out on our behalf, and He alone has promised that they are all for our good.

"Remember the scripture for the day that says, 'To man belong the plans of the heart, but from the Lord comes the reply of the tongue. All a man's ways seem innocent to him, but motives are weighed by the Lord.' That's in Proverbs 16:1-2 (BSB)."

The group stirred at that point, preparing to leave.

"See you guys, next week!" exclaimed the instructor. "Stay blessed. Remember, God's got it all in direct control. Whatever He said, He alone is able to bring it into fruition!"

With that, the class was dismissed.

Part Four

"Positive and negative are directions that lead to different outcomes. Which direction do you choose?"
~Brenda Murphy~

Wrong Direction

Meredith believed the knowledge and wisdom she kept receiving from her class sessions were priceless! She excitedly said that every time she thought the class involvement couldn't get any better, by the end of the class, she was proven wrong again! In fact, she wished that the class could be extended for another hour.

Over the next several months, Meredith invited everyone she met to the class, sharing with them how much it had been a blessing to her.

Heck, she even invited George, but of course, he declined and responded, "Naw, I'm good. I read my Bible two or three times a week. I am fully mindful of what the Word of God says."

Meredith, thinking about all the really great things happening in her life, felt that she was finally coming into all the beautiful and exciting things she worked so hard for. In her career, private life and with her personal family, she wanted nothing more than to share it with that special someone who could share in her daily happiness.

While these thoughts skipped through her mind, her phone rang. You guessed it—good ole George.

"Hello George," Meredith answered. "How are you doing?"

"Never better." He sounded good.

"Is that so? Do tell. I haven't heard from you in quite a while. What have you been up to?"

"Listen, I have been thinking about you, and I would like to take you to lunch tomorrow if you're free. I mean that's if you would like to go with me."

Thinking what a lovely gesture, Meredith replied. "Why George, that's a lovely idea. Sure, I'd love to. When and where? I could meet you there if you would like."

George cleared his throat quickly. "Oh no, no, no. I will stop by your office and pick you up. It wouldn't be a problem at all."

Meredith found herself getting pretty excited about the invite. She decided to overlook all the previous unanswered mysteries she felt in the past concerning George's behavior during their outings together. In the midst of it all, Meredith made a conscious decision to let her guard down—allow the moments with George to run their course. What could it hurt?

The next day, George texted Meredith and asked for the address of her building so he could pick her up. Not thinking anything about it, Meredith rattled off the address and informed George she'd wait outside for him.

However, Meredith got distracted by a business call in her office that took longer than she expected. Before long, she realized George had been outside, waiting for her for over an hour. Or so she thought.

Finishing up with her call, Meredith heard her name being called. She turned around to see George standing in her office, armed with a beautiful bouquet of three dozen long-stem, yellow roses and an incredible box of chocolates.

Completely swept off her feet, she said, "Oh George, you shouldn't have."

George smiled from ear-to-ear. "Oh sweetheart, you don't know it, but this is only the beginning of great times ahead. The power of positive thinking is amazing. Are you ready to go?"

With a big smile, Meredith said, "I guess so. Let me get my purse."

Lunch was great, and the two had a fabulous time. During lunch they caught up on things happening for them in their careers and personal lives. Then the topic of holidays rolled around and how each of them would be spending their time and with whom.

Meredith shared, "I don't have family around, so I'll would either go home to see my parents, or perhaps I'll just stay home and enjoy a safe, quite holiday alone. That's what I did for the last several years. I'm fine with either one." She took a sip of her drink. "This year has been moving like a whirlwind. Some time alone would allow me an opportunity to catch up. At the moment, though, any holiday plans aren't set in stone. How about you? Any specific plans?"

"Well, now that you've asked, I wouldn't mind spending the holiday with my special friend. I mean there's no real reason why two available people could not share the holiday with each other. Even if it means just being friends, right?"

Meredith thought to herself, well, I suppose not. I mean we are both clear about just being friends and nothing more. "I'll think about it," she said. "The holiday is still a couple of months away. Let's just leave it at that for now and not try to rush things, okay?"

George, with a big flashy smile, said, "Yes, sure!"

Back at the office after lunch, Meredith's co-workers were excited to find out about the mysterious man who took her to lunch in such high fashion.

Meredith, desperately trying to turn down the volume on the spotlight, said, "Oh, he's just a friend from the single's ministry I have been attending."

Her co-workers all laughed. "Yeah, right. Single's ministry, okay. And how long has this been happening?"

"Look guys, this wasn't a date or anything. He simply asked me to lunch, and I said yes. That's all."

"Um hmmm," one of them said, eyeing the roses and chocolates. "We should all have a good-looking friend like that."

Meanwhile, Meredith really enjoyed the beautiful bouquet. It had been a long time since someone had thought of her in that manner, and privately, she was impressed with his kindness. She thought, not bad. Who knows? Maybe this could move forward into something more meaningful.

She recalled the quotes from her last Bible study class. Drucker's words played in her brain.

"Plans are only good intentions unless they immediately degenerate into hard work."

"The only thing we know about the future is that it will be different."

Meredith inhaled deeply and said, "Who knows? This just may be worth a try."

"To think negatively is like taking a drug that weakens you."

~Remez Sasson~

Missed Exit Not Too Late To Turn Around

Meredith and George were talking by phone quite a bit during the next couple months on their own terms. Not referring to themselves as boyfriend and girlfriend or significant others. In fact, they both agreed to no labels at all—just to enjoy each other's company with no strings attached.

Everything appeared easy breezy. They both were happy in their own spaces, and honestly, by all intents and purposes, when they were in each other's company, they both simply chose to focus on the moment.

Having thought about George's earlier request to spend Thanksgiving together as friends, Meredith believed they could do so. George seemed to have accepted the fact that their friendship could never be anything more than just that—friends.

She decided to call George up and invite him to her house for Thanksgiving. He was beyond excited and told her so.

He excitedly said, "I cannot wait. You have totally made my day. Oh boy, this is going to be a great holiday for me and hopefully for the both of us."

Days passed quickly, leading up to the Thanksgiving holiday. Everywhere Meredith turned, there was something special in the air. People in general were smiling, happy, being kind to one another. All of a sudden it appeared all was right in the world.

Co-workers planned trips out of town, family gatherings happened more frequently during the week leading up to the holiday, and people seemed more relaxed in anticipation of the holiday season.

During that time, Meredith let her guard down more and became more at ease around George. The week of Thanksgiving arrived, and she found herself breaking out her family's traditional recipes, baking all the favorite childhood deserts. She reminisced about what life was like for her as a child, smiling both inwardly and outwardly.

The morning of Thanksgiving was spent with excitement in the kitchen. Meredith was not able to distinguish between whether her excitement stemmed from Thanksgiving Day itself or that she was spending it with George, her friend, whom she was growing quite fond of.

She told herself that on this day, she would not waste time being overly cautious but rather spend it grateful that she had someone who was excited about sharing the special day with her. Inside, she was thankful for George's friendship and had always told him so.

Around noon on Thanksgiving Day, Meredith texted George her home address and invited him over around 3:00 p.m. for dinner and to watch the football game afterwards. Secretly, she could not wait to see him in person.

Excitement filled George's voice. "I can't wait to see you soon. Should I bring anything special for dinner? Perhaps wine, if you'd like."

Meredith replied, "Sure. That sounds great. White wine

is my favorite. See you soon."

George arrived around 2:45 p.m. "I hope you don't mind. I didn't want to be late for what I deem a very special occasion. Spending Thanksgiving with my special friend, I don't want to waste a moment of it."

Meredith smiled. "Oh George, you seemed to always know the right words to say. Please come in."

After dinner, both Meredith and George settled in for the games and enjoyed their glasses of wine. Things appeared normal between the two of them. Nothing weird happened or was said, and surprisingly enough, George was on his best behavior, which was interesting to Meredith. She was not 100% sure he would be.

As the evening continued, somehow the conversation lead to Christmas traditions and putting up Christmas trees on or after the Thanksgiving holiday. George suddenly got the idea to ask Meredith if she thought about getting a Christmas tree that year.

Meredith replied, "No, I actually had not thought that far in advance."

"Well, I think that you should. I know of this little country farm about an hour's drive from here that starts early to display their Christmas trees that I would like to take you to see; who knows, maybe we can get a cup of hot chocolate and walk around now come on. I'll take you to purchase one today. Let's go get your coat."

Meredith giggling a little said, "Oh George, don't be silly. You don't have to do that."

He grinned from ear-to-ear. "No worries. It will be my pleasure. Now come on. Let's go!"

Out the door they went, acting like two high schoolers

on their first date. George drove, and they listened to Christmas music all the way to the Christmas tree farm to get Meredith her first live Christmas tree.

On the drive there, Meredith said. "George, this is really special. I never had a live tree before."

"Everyone should have a live tree, and it makes me happy to put a smile on your face." When George reached out for Meredith's hand to hold during the drive, surprisingly, she allowed it.

While they had a great time selecting the perfect tree, they also took the time to share nice cups of hot chocolate and chatting away. Even though both parties were having a good time, Meredith didn't want to press her luck further and ruin the evening.

Toward the end of the night, Meredith said, "All good things must come to an end, don't you think?" At the moment, Meredith really was enjoying the time with George, but she was afraid to allow herself to get carried away.

George stared into her eyes. "Yeah, I suppose so. But you know, it doesn't have to." He blushed. "I'm sorry. I am not sure where that came from. My apologies."

For the first time, Meredith could see in George's eyes that he was serious about these moments they were experiencing together. The truth of the matter, she was feeling those same emotions herself.

"No need to apologize, George. Let's get the tree into the car, and then we can go home."

"Would you like to stop for coffee on the way home?" George asked.

Meredith immediately said, "No, I think we have had enough fun for one day. Just take me home, please."

"Sure thing," George said.

In the car, Meredith didn't realize the effect a couple glasses of wine had on her, but tiredness overtook her. She decided to lay her head back on the headrest and simply close her eyes for a minute. Listening to the smooth music, she dozed off.

Suddenly, opening up her eyes and sensing that they should have reached her street by now, she sat straight up in the car.

She yelled, "George, where are we? What are you doing? This is not my exit. You passed my exit. Where are you taking me? How did this happen?"

George, sounding panicked, tried to calm Meredith down and offer a satisfactory answer. He quickly said, "I apologize. I guess I just wasn't paying much attention to where I was going and inadvertently missed our exit. I'm sorry. It was not intentional."

"Really?"

"Meredith, please let me explain. I sincerely apologize," he begged. "Please hear me out. I was caught up in the moment of being with you, the music, the atmosphere, and I guess, I just missed your exit. I'll turn around at the next one. Okay?"

Meredith kept quiet. Waiting for the next exit. In Meredith's mind, she was over it entirely. At the moment, all she wanted to do was to get home safely and rid of George.

"Be sober-minded; be watchful. Your adversary the devil prowls around like a roaring lion, seeking someone to devour. Resist him, firm in your faith, knowing that the same kinds of suffering are being experienced by your brotherhood throughout the world."

~1 Peter 5:8-9 (ESV)

Under the Wrong Influence

In that moment, Meredith was struggling to make sense of exactly what was happening.

At first, she and George were having a great evening together, enjoying each other's company. No more. Meredith panicked. Hysteria set in. The night of terror flashed through her mind. The same horror. Someone trying to hurt her. George? She couldn't explain it. But the same fear grasped her, held her in its clutches. She didn't like it.

How had the evening turned so sour? At one point, they were relaxed, having a great time together, and totally enjoying each other's company. Watching the football games and drinking wine, then Christmas tree shopping together. She didn't get it. How could the evening end up being so tense and unpredictable?

It didn't matter to Meredith at that point. She just wanted the moment to be over, vowing in her mind that she would never see George again.

Never.

After they arrived at her home, there was still the issue

of getting the Christmas tree out of George's car and into Meredith's house. By then, she was definitely uncomfortable with him spending any more time alone with her.

At first, Meredith encouraged George to just take the tree home with him. She no longer had any interest in it. "Please just take it and go home now. I want to be alone, and I don't want to see you again. Ever."

Annoyance laced George's voice. "Meredith, you're overreacting. This is a simple case of misjudgment. You're taking this a little too far to the left. I already sincerely apologized. For what? Getting caught up in the moment?" He took a breath. "I understand you're upset, but this instance certainly should not render me disqualified to ever see you again. Come on. Be reasonable. It was a simple mistake."

Eventually, Meredith calmed down enough to allow George to bring the tree into her house and set it up. Then he was ordered to leave immediately.

She said, "This whole evening spent together may have been my mistake. I should have known better."

George was past being offended. He was hurt and angry at the way Meredith seemed to be manipulating their friendship when it was convenient for her.

Before George left, he turned to Meredith, his silence a heartfelt message he hoped. He genuinely cared for her but was hurt by her over-the-top emotions.

He thought, "I am not a dog you can simply summon to come to you at your beck and call."

After putting the tree in place, she once again shouted at

him. "Good night, George. You can leave now!"

Being the gentleman, he honored her request. On the way out the door, he turned to Meredith one last time. "Are you sure about this?"

"Absolutely," Meredith shouted. "Get out of my house now, please—and lose the address."

Slamming the door behind him as he left, Meredith mumbled to herself, "This is ridiculous. I thought George was more mature than this. What was I thinking? How could he keep assuming there is so much more between us? I have never misled him. I have always been straight forward from the very beginning."

Before going to bed that night, Meredith decided to take a nice long shower and revisit the afternoon in her mind. try to figure out exactly how things got out of control between her and George. Never believing for one moment that she might have played a real role in the upheaval of it all. At that time, she didn't stop to consider George's feelings. She blamed it all on him.

After a shower, Meredith crawled into bed and fell into a deep sleep. Little did she know she was going to have a life-changing dream. One that would set the next few years of her life on a journey filled with various twists and turns. A journey she would never imagine happening to her.

At first, Meredith could not sleep. She spent most of the night tossing and turning. Sighing and frustrated with how her afternoon and evening turned out with George. She could not for the life of her figure out what went wrong.

They had a nice dinner. They laughed and talked and

watched the football game together. They ate dessert, drank wine, and then more wine. Then a little more wine.

Exhausted, Meredith finally drifted off to sleep.

During her sleep, words kept coming to mind, a soft whisper in her dreams. Be sober-minded; be watchful. *Be sober minded; be watchful.* Meredith didn't realize that while she was sleeping, she unconsciously repeated the phrase continually. "Be sober-minded; be watchful."

Turning over in bed, Meredith woke slightly and remembered reading a scripture in 1 Peter 5:8-9 (ESV) "*Be sober-minded; be watchful. Your adversary the devil prowls around like a roaring lion, seeking someone to devour. Resist him, firm in your faith, knowing that the same kinds of suffering are being experienced by your brotherhood throughout the world."*

Still, Meredith kept right on dreaming, unable to see the error perhaps of her ways or her particular role in this episode of her life.

In her dream, Meredith asked, "How? What? What's happening? Why is this happening to me?"

During the dream, Meredith saw herself back in the Bible study classroom, but this time she was asking questions of the leader regarding 1 Peter 5:8-9. She wanted to know exactly what that scripture meant and how she could relate it to her own life.

She clearly heard the leader's response. "Self-mastery ("soberly" in the New King James Version) is self-government or self-control, the foundation of a strong godly life, growth, and producing fruit. If a person cannot govern himself, if he cannot master his passions, he will certainly not have a good relationship with his fellow man or God. His life will probably be marked by major excesses.

"The biblical writers used this word in various ways—to behave in an orderly manner, to be sober, serious, sane, sound-minded, discreet, self-disciplined, prudent, and moderate.

"In context of a person controlling himself, Paul writes, 'For I say, through the grace given to me, to everyone who is among you, not to think of himself more highly than he ought to think, but to think soberly, as God has dealt to each one a measure of faith.' That's in Romans 12:3, the NKJV version, but also look at Titus 2:6 and I Peter 4:7."

Finally, in the dream, the instructor said, "A person who has self-mastery is even-handed, and his passions are under control. He makes proper use of his drives and desires, and his manner of life is not one of extremes. A person reflecting this quality will be making steady progress and growing into the perfectly balanced character of Jesus Christ."

Suddenly, Meredith was awakened by her alarm clock, reeling from what the instructor was teaching her even in her sleep.

Why was he sharing this type of message with her? It felt so real, as if he stood with her that night. She wasn't the one she thought causing the confusion or sending out mixed messages. It was George.

She felt as though up to that point, she had done nothing but be upfront with George, telling him from the very beginning that she wanted nothing more from him than to be his friend—no strings attached. She was positive that hadn't sent out anything contrary to those feelings.

Eager to be back in Bible study class again, Meredith

could barely wait for Wednesday to come. Before the instructor started, she proposed that he elaborate more on the subject of 1 Peter 5:8-9 (ESV) "Be sober-minded; be watchful. Your adversary the devil prowls around like a roaring lion, seeking someone to devour. Resist him, firm in your faith, knowing that the same kinds of suffering are being experienced by your brotherhood throughout the world."

"Gladly," the instructor said. "The grace of God obligates us to these duties in our relationship with others. To conform to them fulfills what Paul means by living with integrity as is found in Titus 2:12.

"Being sober-minded encompasses keeping the commandments, of course, but it also involves such virtues as probity, honesty, goodness, irreproachability, fairness, nobility, and being just and sensitive to another's needs. That includes giving correction in kindness and mercy, as Paul wrote in Galatians 6:1-2."

Meredith quietly said under her breath, "Ouch!"

She thought intently about her last conversation and the words she blurted out to George. She was sure after hearing this statement from the instructor that she was everything but sober-minded.

Ashamed of how she reacted, she thought, "How in the world am I going to face George again after that fiasco?"

By then, others in the class had concerns as well and asked if this could be the topic of discussion instead of what was prepared.

The instructor was delighted and continued with more explanation.

"Looking at Genesis 3:4-7, in verse 4, we find Satan slyly

convincing Eve that God has lied to them by withholding from them the ability to become 'like God, knowing good and evil.' God was being unfair, the old snake argues, keeping them from their potential.

"The passage even suggests that, after hearing this, Eve did not hesitate one bit in making her decision. She took the bait without flinching and ignorantly promoted the interests of Satan by giving the forbidden fruit to her husband."

In some ways, Meredith thought about the importance of thinking for herself and not allowing the personal fears, doubts and phobias that from time to time that were swirling in her head to take charge of her overall perspective. She realized that her life was finally headed in a good direction now, and she didn't want to turn back to anything that had previously held her back.

*"My dear brothers and sisters, take note of this:
Everyone should be quick to listen, slow to speak and
slow to become angry."*
~ James 1:9 (NIV)

Leave No Space Vacant

Over the next two months, Meredith decided to do the necessary soul searching within herself to find out why things were happening in her life the way they were— particularly where George was concerned.

Her intentions were never to send mixed messages, or to build up George's expectations for any kind of future together. Upon reflecting, she could not be 100% sure if she really made herself clear. To be perfectly honest, even if she did, was she speaking from her heart or simply reacting out of a knee-jerk decision she was making in the moment?

Deep inside, she felt badly about how she left things with George, and it didn't help matters that she raised her voice at him the last time they were together. Meredith acknowledged she had perhaps overreacted and in the grand scheme of things, definitely could have responded differently.

In hind sight, she considered the rudeness of her actions. She wasn't sure if her reaction was more from doubts about her true feelings for George or a knee-jerk reaction to fears of him finding out just how much she cared about him deep down.

Rather than stress over whether she was wrong or right,

she decided to make a list of both options. From there, she would be able to move forward successfully with the right approach toward George.

For the pros, Meredith listed handsome, confident, smart, articulate, good career, single, no children, passionate about God, friendly and very approachable—just to name a few.

After putting the pen down she thought, "Well, what's wrong with this picture? I cannot seem to find anything that's not a good fit. What am I thinking?"

When it came to the cons, she quickly listed not a good listener, headstrong, driven, and then she stopped suddenly.

"Wait a minute, am I really being fair? Am I being honest in my conclusion of George?"

Suddenly, her con list read more like personal judgment than actual truth.

Meredith found herself unable to separate whether she was speaking of her own personal fears and doubts. Or were the things she was listing about George really accurate? She began questioning her motives in the situation.

At some point, Meredith came to the conclusion that she had to allow herself to feel the real truth about what was going on. She could no longer hide behind a mask.

She concluded that even if George was the issue, she knew she had to handle the situation on a more mature, kinder level. Realizing that she more than likely overreacted, was that a good reason to dismiss someone so quickly?

Until that moment, Meredith was 100% sure she had always been upfront with George. She didn't believe she was leading him on in any manner. However, in her heart of hearts, she questioned if that was her nerves talking as she tried to deflect how she really felt about George—from the first time she saw him.

Sure, she admired him, might go as far to say that she liked him a little. Okay, she even enjoyed his company. But was it... Could it be more than that on her end? Dare she say that she was falling for George but not ready to allow herself to acknowledge it?

Let me interject something in this story. George wasn't just a nice guy, looking for a "girlfriend" that he could simply spend time with and have a good time. He himself was a changed man looking for a woman that he could have a godly relationship with.

He was looking for a special person that he would be proud to introduce as his wife and soulmate. George knew fully well what it was like to simply be in a relationship going nowhere. After he had been introduced to Meredith, he knew she was the only one for him. But he was willing to wait because "she, Meredith, was worth every bit of it."

Now, back to Meredith.

Until then, she was still figuring things out for herself and George. She thought, "Everything would be perfect if George could only accept the friendship for what it was and nothing more. Every time they spent any time together, why did he get the wrong impression and automatically push for more? In her mind, that was what made her balk at a chance for anything more in the first place."

At the end of the day, could all this pushback be because she knew in her heart of heart that she was falling in love and could not help herself from moving forward? That thought terrified her, although she didn't know why.

Realizing that at some point that she needed to make a

decision about where all of this was going, Meredith went back and forth in her reasoning and convictions, trying to understand her anger at times when George seemingly overstepped his boundaries. Even though she did not appreciate his method of operation, she was still willing to be friends with him. Why?

Sometimes, Meredith felt as though George disrespected her wishes and concerns and simply took matters into his own hands. At other times, she believed he was kind, gentle and caring and just trying to show his interest in pursuing a possible real, meaningful and healthy relationship with her when she was ready.

At the moment, she couldn't bear the thought of George being upset with her, and maybe never hearing from him again. By then, she was too afraid to reach out because she didn't want to endure the rejection if he didn't want to hear from her again. So she did absolutely nothing about it and decided to wait for him to make the next move.

Her friends at work mentioned the lack of enthusiasm in Meredith and occasionally inquired about her sad countenance.

She quickly responded, "I don't want to talk about it right now. It's personal."

No matter how much Meredith tried to work things out on her terms, she could not figure out why she was so suddenly confused regarding the casual friendship between George and herself.

Meredith thought out loud, "Oh my goodness. I really don't know where things went wrong."

Unexpectedly, she found herself in a position she never in her entire life imagined. At a crossroads with her emotions regarding George, she didn't know exactly how to handle it either.

Was she asking or expecting too much? Was she just playing hard to get? Was she, in reality, imagining her life with George in it but allowing her fears to overwhelm her? Had she simply ended the potential relationship before ever giving it a chance to grow?

On the one hand, she imagined herself with George in her life, even possibly as her significant other. However, she sometimes felt a disconnection between them whenever they could not agree on the same things. For Meredith, connection was important—if their relationship was going to possibly move forward into more than the friends' zone. If not, why bother to continue moving forward?

After all, they needed to be on the same page. In her mind, more often than not, they were not. It was as if Meredith wanted George to simply follow her lead and not overstep her well-drawn boundaries.

While all that logic sounded good in theory, Meredith realized, deep down in her heart, when she imagined George not being in her life, she missed him terribly. She desperately wished things had not ended so badly. She was very embarrassed to see George again in person.

Regardless, she actually missed hearing his strong, masculine voice, the way he always made her feel special when she was in his presence. She acknowledged that George always showed nothing but love, kindness, compassion and excitement in his eyes when they spent time together.

More confused than ever, Meredith determined to forget about George—as if she could. Something had to give. This indecision and confusion made her crazy. And it had to stop. Somehow.

As Meredith pondered these things, she cried out to God for understanding. But He remained silent. Meredith didn't understand that God was supplying her with the answers and healing she needed. Instead, she was blinded by emotional fears and doubts.

God was showing her that if she willingly let down her guard and trusted herself fully in His hands, He would personally walk her through each doubt. Not only would He help her come through them, but to be an overcomer of them all.

Meredith had to realize that sometimes in life, we are adamant about holding others to a standard higher than the one we surrender to. In other words, secretively she was asking George to complete all the standards she felt he needed to perform before she would be willing to announce to the world that their "friendship" had officially moved forward to the next level.

At that point, Meredith realized she had to either risk losing George and their friendship possibly forever or come clean with him. She was already in love with him, but fearful of acknowledging it.

Yes, she was madly in love with George.

Part Five

"Therefore, since we are surrounded by such a huge crowd of witnesses to the life of faith, let us strip off every weight that slows us down, especially the sin that so easily trips us up. And let us run with endurance the race God has set before us."

~Hebrews 12:1-2 (NLT)

Spiritual Identity Crisis

It had been literally months since Meredith felt like attending the weekly Bible study—the one she had been super excited about attending. With the struggle of personal emotions involving her on-again, off-again relationship with George, she was suddenly not totally sure about anything.

For some strange reason, at the thought of attending the weekly study, Meredith found herself ashamed because of how she lashed out at George. Worse, because she didn't apologize in person or by phone.

One Wednesday, Meredith felt compelled to go alone, not with Sharon. She didn't want to talk to anyone—just listen. She hoped that in so doing, she would be able to hear a special message or receive direction as to how she should proceed in her personal journey.

After reaching the class, Meredith sheepishly rushed in and took a seat on the back row as though she were a spectator. She was desperately searching for answers to help her move forward with life and try to get back on track.

Smiling on the outside but miserable on the inside, Meredith wanted to feel confident again and assured she was moving in the right direction. Ready to begin, the instructor for the day opened the class with a word of prayer. Distracted by her thoughts, one phrase caught Meredith's attention.

"…and speak clearly to those seeking direction today."

Meredith looked up half-expecting the teacher to look in her eyes. He didn't, but he definitely had Meredith's attention.

After the prayer, the instructor posed a question. "Are any of you here today struggling, indecisive in thought and follow through? Do you fully understand your identity as a Christian? Not how you see yourself, but as God sees you?"

Meredith almost fainted.

She could hardly contain herself, fighting not to scream out loud, "Yes, yes, yes!"

Using her better judgment, she held it all in.

The leader continued. "In his book, *Spiritual Identity*, Brother Larry Silver unveils 16 clear and compelling aspects of the spiritual identity of every Christian, straight from the Bible.

"He emphasizes that our identity isn't something we strive for, but something we are. The practical implications of this understanding are mind-blowing. By embracing your true identity, as described in *Spiritual Identity*, you will reap even greater joy, confidence, and impact for the kingdom of God and for eternity.

"In a review, Dean Jones writes, 'It is no worthiness of our own that gives us authority in the spiritual arena, and Larry gives us chapter and verse to solidify the reality of that truth.' Embrace this message and your life will be profoundly changed, forever."

Meredith was 100% sure the message could not have been an accident. She knew it had to be for her. Who else could know her heart and thoughts in this particular subject matter but God?

Oh my goodness, could it possibly be that God was trying to get her attention? The thought left her shaking slightly.

As the teacher continued, he reiterated that a **spiritual identity** crisis is not really a crisis. It is the conscious self, coming to terms with the **spiritual** self, living in a material world, encountering external forces, pressures and influences.

"Take, for instance, the scripture reading of Hebrews 12:1-2," he said.

"Therefore, since we are surrounded by such a huge crowd of witnesses to the life of faith, let us strip off every weight that slows us down, especially the sin that so easily trips us up.

"And let us run with endurance the race God has set before us. We do this by keeping our eyes on Jesus, the Champion who initiates and perfects our faith. Because of the joy awaiting Him, He endured the cross, disregarding its shame. Now He is seated in the place of honor beside God's throne." (NLT)

"If you will only take a few minutes to simply look around in today's society, you can see the church becoming a lot like the world in many respects. The fact of the matter is we are all humans.

"But that can't be used as a basis for choosing to live in sin as a Christian. In Romans 6, Paul, under the inspiration of the Holy Spirit writes to us that if we are born again, our old man is dead. Sin should no longer have dominion over us."

Meredith remained a babe in Christ—not because she was unable to read and self-interpret her understanding of God's Word. She remained a babe because she struggled with letting go of how she perceived her understanding. She couldn't grasp the fact that God's will does not always make sense to mankind. Although God doesn't always make sense, He makes wisdom. Therefore, according to Proverbs 4:7 (NIV), we should get the wisdom first and make it a priority "The beginning of wisdom is this: Get wisdom. Though it cost all you have, get understanding."

Meredith, like many, tried to reduce somehow what God was saying to her level of understanding, rather than respecting and embracing that our God knows all and is 100% accurate in all His doing.

Her unwillingness to do so brought about confusion and fears. Therefore, she was unable to put all the pieces of the "Spiritual Identity" puzzle together. She needed a lot more understandable clarification.

The instructor continued with the lesson. "If you're born again and struggle with the weakness of the flesh nature and desire sin, then know that you don't fully understand or know your spiritual identity. For example, when you were born, your mom was probably asked what she would name her new baby.

"In much the same way, you were born again as a child of God and given a new identity in Christ. Look back to 2 Corinthians 5:17. When we don't understand what it means to walk in our new nature or spiritual identity in Christ, we have a tendency to identify with our old ways and desires."

The instructor searched the group's faces. "The remedy to dying to your old carnal or fleshly ways is to continue to walk by faith. There is absolutely no other possible way. What does that mean? You no longer listen to what your heart, lusts, the world, or Satan is saying. Rather, you adhere to the Word of God and the leading of the Holy Spirit.

"As you begin to walk by faith, and you discover your new identity apart from sin, your fleshly desires will scream, 'Stop this faith stuff. I need some attention.'"

The group chuckled, some a bit uncomfortably.

Continuing, the teacher added, "You will know when your old man is getting the attention of your heart. For at those times, you will look at what walking by faith is keeping you from."

At that point, a small light bulb moment happened for Meredith. She never once looked at herself or her thoughts in that manner before. While this was all new for her, she was intrigued to learn more.

The instructor continued, "If this describes where you are spiritually, then you should know that you have gotten to the place in your faith walk that Hebrews 12:1-2 addresses.

"When our flesh nature and worldly desires tell us what we're missing due to trusting and following Jesus, then we have to make some tough decisions. Please note that some or most of those decisions will not be easy, or at least in your mind, necessary. You may even try to deny, fight or hide those sins or emotions while opting to believe that you can handle them all on your own."

Meredith fidgeted, uncomfortable.

"But if we make the correct choices, we'll find that it gets easier when our faith grows and we walk consistently in our new identities. The more we relinquish ourselves unto the Lord, we will better walk in personal victories."

Just then, a student in the class raised his hand sheepishly. "Can you possibly explain just how that is supposed to happen?"

"Great question," the instructor replied. "It will become easier for two reasons. As you say 'no' to the old man and 'yes' to the Lord's will for your life, the old man is being crucified by the Word daily. As a result, you will walk in more **authority over that flesh nature** that once ruled you."

He paused, letting the words settle.

"This will make it much easier for you to say no to the flesh and the cares of this world. But if you get to a place in your walk with Christ where it seems like He is asking more of you than you are receiving from Him, then know that is the time to seek Him more.

"Remember, you must decrease, and Jesus must increase. If you decrease, and yet don't pursue Him more, then the flesh's nature will grow back stronger. In other words, we must replace our old ways of doing things with the new and improved method and mannerism of Christ."

By the time the Bible study ended, Meredith's head was spinning with knowledge and biblical principles. She had lots to think about and pray over. What she did realize was that she wanted to know more about Jesus and to grow in Him.

That must become the most important thought in her mind and heart.

"For our struggle is not against flesh and blood, but against the rulers, against the authorities, against the powers of this dark world and against the spiritual forces of evil in the heavenly realms."
~Ephesians 6:12 (NIV)

Faceless Stalker

Finding herself at home on the weekend with ample "me" time on her hands, Meredith, an avid reader, was given some mystery books by a previous client to read for her good pleasure.

Looking through the stash of books given to her, Meredith was suddenly intrigued by one particular book title. For some bizarre reason, Meredith found herself being drawn to this mystery book entitled *Faceless Stalker*.

While intrigued by its title, she was also a little nervous about reading its content. Nevertheless, she could not bring herself to pass it up. She thought, "It couldn't hurt to read a few pages just for grins, right?"

At the very outset of reading, Meredith found herself immediately drawn into this dark web of learning exactly what a faceless stalker was all about. Feeling she should stop while she was ahead, she felt drawn to know more. So she kept reading.

According to the author, Meredith was learning that a faceless stalker can assume the form of a Medium humanoid at will but requires 10 uninterrupted minutes to alter its body.

Performing this transformation is somewhat painful, but the faceless stalker can maintain its new form indefinitely once it has achieved the conversion. It can change back to its true form as a swift action and gains a plus two morale bonus on attack rolls, damage rolls, skill checks, and saving throws for one round after it does so.

Faceless stalkers retain their innate abilities when they assume their new form and do not gain any of those belonging to the creature they mimic. A faceless stalker gains a plus ten bonus on disguise checks when they are used in conjunction with this ability.

Faceless stalkers, in their natural form, have no discernible facial features. It gains a plus four bonus on saving throws made to resist attacks or effects that target the senses. This includes gaze attacks, odor-based attacks, sonic attacks and similar attacks. This bonus applies to illusions.

Ugothols (as faceless stalkers call themselves) are one of the many tools created and then discarded by the aboleths in their long war against the surface dwellers.

Scorned by their former masters when the scheme for which they were designed unraveled, the faceless stalkers fled into swamps, marshes, or any other dark, wet places they could find—the closest they could come to the aquatic cities they once considered home.

Originally designed to serve as spies that could walk uncontested among the air-breathing races, faceless stalkers adopt new forms by reshaping their skin and contorting their rubbery bodies.

This painful process takes approximately 10 uninterrupted minutes—an Ugothols typically seeks a private place to do it, avoiding even others of its own kind.

The sensation of returning to its true form is quite exhilarating and results in a momentary burst of euphoria.

Faceless stalkers cannot digest solid food even when in the form of a creature with a mouth. Instead, they subsist on liquids, including blood. In their natural forms, they have three hollow tongues which they use to penetrate and lap blood from their victims.

Since they have no particular skill at grappling foes, most Ugothols wait until a victim is helpless or asleep before attempting to drink its blood—although the best is when a victim is helpless but conscious during the process, so that the faceless stalker can "play with its food" by having grisly and cruel conversations with it.

From time-to-time, Meredith privately continued to struggle with the confidence within herself. She didn't understand where the doubts came from. She had never experienced that problem before.

In her earlier years, she was extremely confident in her strength and abilities to accomplish whatever she set her mind to. It appeared that whatever she touched turned to gold.

No longer. Meredith was struggling in areas where she never experienced challenges before, and she was becoming increasingly anxious, nervous, distracted and off kilter. She was beginning to second-guess herself in just about every major decision she made.

She was afraid to seek help, afraid of how she might appear to the public's view of her if they thought she was not the "confident, secure" person she always portrayed herself to be.

The image that others saw of her was everything. If she

thought for one moment that others were possibly judging her, she would be sorely disappointed and hurt. Also, she would be unwilling to face or accept that as her new reality.

Over a long Labor Day weekend, Meredith found herself out of sorts. She wasn't necessarily sad. However, she wasn't exactly jovial either. She wished she could sincerely get a do-over with George so they could put all the bad stuff behind them and move forward.

Daily, she racked her brain, but she still could not readily place a finger on what was causing her situation to grow worse. She knew she wasn't the same person as before George came into her life. Since he left, she felt incomplete.

Over the next several weeks, Meredith held her Bible close and read every chance she got, realizing she needed to know more about how to handle life challenges in a more precise fashion.

Admittedly, she did not always fully understand what she was reading in terms of interpretation. Yet each time she read the Word of God, she seemed to be in a better space afterwards.

During those weeks, Meredith began reading and meditating upon Ephesians 6:12. *"For we wrestle not against flesh and blood…"* (KJV) Intrigued by it, Meredith decided to call upon Sharon, asking her to walk through what the scripture meant by that statement.

Sharon was more than willing to provide as much insight about the verse as possible. "Well, our conflict is not with men. The Bible is very clear about using the term "flesh and blood," which is usually a symbol of our weakness, therefore denoting that our opponents are not weak mortals, but powers of a far more formidable order."

"That makes sense," Meredith said. "But what are those powers, and how does that affect us?"

"We war or fight against something far greater—against the principalities, against the powers of a bigger force. If you will take a look at Ephesians 1:21, it says, although all of these, evil as well as good, have been put under Christ the Head, today, we are still warring with a greater intensity. Every day, we are warring against the world-rulers of this world darkness. 'World-rulers' denotes the extent of the dominion of these invisible foes.

"The term is applied only to the rulers of the most widely extended tracts. There is no part of the globe to which their influence does not extend, and where their dark rule does not show itself. You might want to look up Luke 4:6."

"I'm writing down these verses so I can look them up later," Meredith assured her friend. "Go on, please."

"This darkness expressively signifies the element and the results of their rule. It also contrasts with Christ's servants, who are children of light—equivalent to order, knowledge, purity, joy, peace, and such, while the element of the devil and his servants is darkness—equivalent to confusion, ignorance, crime, terror, strife, and all misery."

"So the powers basically in this verse refer to Satan and his followers?"

"Yes, Meredith. We continue to wrestle against the spiritual hosts of wickedness in the heavenly places like the verse says. The natural meaning, though questioned by some, is that either these hosts of wickedness have their residence in heavenly places, or that these places are the scene of our conflict with them."

"Okay." Thinking about Sharon's explanation intrigued

Meredith.

"In Ephesians 3:6, it is said that while 'we have been seated with Christ in heavenly places,' the reference is to the spiritual experience of His people. In spirit, they are at the gate of heaven, where their hearts are full of heavenly thoughts and feelings. The statement before us is that, even in such places, amid their most fervent experiences or their most sublime services, they are subject to the attacks of the spirits of wickedness.

"In other words, we can never be off our guard to watch, fight and pray, because the surrounding evilness is always desiring to take us out and to render harm unto us. Each day we must be careful to ask the divine protection of our God to watch over us and see us through the day safely—to keep us from all hurt, harm and danger."

As they continued the conversation, Meredith had one thought. Why did the enemy continually want to fight them? What was his problem?

"The thief comes only to steal and kill and destroy; I have come that they may have life, and have it to the full."

~John 10:10 (NIV)

Kill, Steal & Destroy

As Meredith shared her question, Sharon continued. "There is one thing that is definite. If you are breathing, we have an enemy that is tracking our every move at all times. It does not matter who you are, where you live, where you work or even who you may think you are. Make no mistake, you are being followed in every sense of the word."

By then, Meredith was just starting to get the idea that perhaps all the previous turn of events were purposefully staged or aligned for her life. As they ended their conversation, she reconsidered specific things leading up to that point.

She opened a Bible app on her phone to read the verse in different versions.

She first opened up the American King James Version. *"The thief comes not, but for to steal, and to kill, and to destroy: I am come that they might have life, and that they might have it more abundantly."*

In the American Standard Version, she read, *"The thief cometh not, but that he may steal, and kill, and destroy: I came that they may have life, and may have it abundantly."*

Meredith, like most of us, was still growing in her faith, still seeking God for more clarity and understanding of what it meant to grow closer to Him and rest in His presence. That way, when the attacks of the enemy came against her like a mighty flood, she had directions about getting to that Secret Place in God.

One day, as Meredith was holed up in her bedroom, daydreaming about how her life got to where she was, she felt drawn to the book of Isaiah for some interesting reason. She opened her New King James Version Bible to Isaiah 59:19.

"So shall they fear the name of the Lord from the west, and his glory from the rising of the sun; when the enemy comes in like a flood, the Spirit of the Lord will lift up a standard against him."

Seeking the face of God for a greater understanding of this subject matter, Meredith did some homework and came to fresh understanding. In the verse, she saw that when people start doing the right thing (being in awe and reverence of God), that is when the promise comes into effect.

The enemy does not need to come in like a flood when people are not honoring and serving God. They are already accomplishing his purposes. It is only when people are becoming dangerous to the enemy of our souls that they need to fight what is going on.

Still not being able to shake herself from the previous night's events, Meredith prayed, "Lord, please help me understand the spiritual nature of this attack on my life."

As she began to dig deeper into the study of John 10:10, the first thing she noticed was she needed to understand that when anyone comes under attack, it is spiritual in source and nature. A study caused her to stop and pay attention, especially because the words rang true to her.

Many times we are tempted to look at the circumstances or people and view them as the enemy. They may be tools of the enemy, but your enemy is not people, finances, or obstacles of any kind. The cause is a spiritual agenda that wants to stop you from doing the things you are doing that are infringing on the kingdom of darkness.

But the enemy is spiritual, not physical. While he can keep us from being focused on the matter at hand, he will continue to send distractions from all angles to derail us from God's truth that not only sets us free but also keeps us fluid in His perfect will for our lives.

As she continued to study, she came to the conclusion that she needed to understand the weapons of her warfare were not physical but spiritual (2 Corinthians 10:4).

As Meredith sat studying, she heard a revelation, as if the Holy Spirit spoke to her heart.

"If you are going to fight a spiritual battle, you have to use the weapons that work in that realm. These weapons are prayer, fasting, and the Word of God. When you are in a spiritual battle, you need to increase your prayer time, skip some meals, and get into the Word of God for both direction and the building of your faith. Don't try to win this battle with human reasoning and methods. Let the Lord win this battle for you. Let His Holy Spirit lift up the 'battle standard' against him."

Even though there was still so much Meredith needed to learn about spiritual warfare, she would have to learn some of it while walking it out in the midst of her warfare.

Meredith further learned that a standard was an old English word used in battle. When a standard or flag was raised, it signaled all the troops to rally at that point. "The Hebrew word 'Nuwc' means to fly (to the attack) on horseback," she read.

In that moment, Meredith's was willing to allow the Holy Spirit to be the one that lifted up the standard to repel the enemy of doubt and confusion swirling around in her mind. She learned in her studies that she must easily be willing to give up before the battle was over.

One of the greatest temptations and mistakes she had to face was her propensity of giving up when things were getting frustrating for her. She was learning that many times the battle rages the fiercest when the victory is almost won. She had to learn that this was the time of digging her heels in, squaring her shoulders, and fixing her focus upon the Lord—period.

She needed to understand that the enemy of our souls has an intense hatred for anyone that follows Jesus wholeheartedly. He will not just lay over like a beat dog and expose his neck at the first sign of battle. He goes around like a roaring lion, not a whipped puppy. She looked at 1 Peter 5:8 again.

He was looking to devour her. She had no doubt about the truth of that statement.

Meredith had to declare and decree that when things got hot for her, when they got tough, when they got scary, not to give up. She had to learn as a believer that her Redeemer draws near. (Luke 21:28)

As she continued to seek God and hunger and thirst for more wisdom and understanding of how this battle thing worked, she realized that gaining a better understanding regarding the battle meant she must understand that sometimes, if not all times, the battle in our lives costs dearly.

Most have a concept of a lossless victory. Meredith

understood that. Something we notoriously call failure. Warfare in the physical realm costs lives and resources. So too, in the spiritual realm, it might cost her. The price of taking up your cross and following Jesus.

The more Meredith studied the Word of God, she saw the Apostle Paul as an excellent example of how spiritual warfare cost Christians. If she were to continue following Jesus, it was going to cost her as well.

She turned to 2 Corinthians in her NKJV Bible. Paul was beaten, stoned, imprisoned, left for dead, famished, etc. All those things were the cost of the war the enemy brought against him. But he learned a crucial lesson in all of it that he recorded for in 2 Corinthians 12:7-10. She read the passage again.

"And lest I should be exalted above measure by the abundance of the revelations, a thorn in the flesh was given to me, a messenger of Satan to buffet me, lest I be exalted above measure. Concerning this thing, I pleaded with the Lord three times that it might depart from me. And He said to me, 'my grace is sufficient for you, for my strength is made perfect in weakness.' Therefore, most gladly I will rather boast in my infirmities, that the power of Christ may rest upon me. Therefore I take pleasure in infirmities, in reproaches, in needs, in persecutions, in distresses, for Christ's sake. For when I am weak, then I am strong."

Meredith had to learn that it was most important to allow Christ to be her strength when the enemy comes in like a flood. She didn't know it until then, but she was being sought by the enemy. She had to allow God to guide her.

To win this battle, she must continue to lean and depend upon the Lord for total direction and guidance for everyday life. She could not afford to ever take matters into her own natural hands.

She said to herself, "God desires to lead, guide and protect us 24/7. He is able, more than enough, and capable of keeping us safe at all times."

"Your word is a lamp for my feet, a light on my path."
~ Psalm 119:105 (NIV)

Spiritual Lineup

Meredith had been so wrapped up in studying God's Word, having her mind renewed and rewired to things of the spiritual realm more than the corporate world.

Little did she know that her appetite was no longer lusting as much for natural things. She was hungry for more in-depth wisdom and understanding of God's Word and insight for her life's journey. Day and night she was learning how to meditate on what was next for her.

She could not believe how much she was growing and soaring through the reading and searching of the Word of God concerning her life. One minute, she seemingly had so little knowledge of who He was to her. Heck, for that matter, there were days she would venture to ask whether He even knew who she was.

Her personal journey was causing a dramatic detour in her life far away from the corporate cares and overwhelmingness of everyday agendas. Meredith could not wait to go back to Bible study to share and learn with friends she was accustomed to studying the Word of God with.

While she was thankful for the business she was building, she realized she was absolutely nothing and that it was worthless without God as her spiritual partner within the business. She was coming into the knowledge that without God, she could accomplish absolutely nothing.

She needed more, wanted more. She had to have more—thirsty and hungry for more than what she had in her life. Something within her was crying out for more, deeper, Greater than she could imagine. She needed Jesus at levels unknown to her senses.

In class that day, Meredith could barely contain herself when the teacher prayed, "God, please give us clarity within our class today. Open up our spiritual minds to receive greater from your Word. We need more of You and none of us. Thank You, now Father, for we believe that we have received of You today!"

Then the instructor said, "Let's focus our hearts on something God placed upon my heart to talk about today. If you have your Bibles with you, please join me in our study by turning to the passage of scripture located in Psalm 119:105-108."

Pages rustled as several opened up their Bibles.

A group member read, using a NIV Bible. "Your word is a lamp for my feet, a light on my path. I have taken an oath and confirmed it, that I will follow your righteous laws. I have suffered much; preserve my life, LORD, according to your word. Accept, LORD, the willing praise of my mouth, and teach me your laws."

The teacher asked, "What does that statement mean? 'Thy word is a lamp unto my feet?' This is a mouthful. This is vital. This is imperative that we are not just walking around to and fro, but we should ask God every day to order and direct our steps. Then wait on Him to do so." He paused.

"But to understand that the Word of God is a lamp unto our feet and a light for our pathway. To direct me in all my doubts and difficulties, and to comfort me in all my fears and distresses."

The instructor continued to lecture. "I have sworn, and will perform it — I have solemnly vowed, and by God's grace will fulfil our vow that we will keep His righteous judgments. His commands, which are consonant to the eternal rules of equity, and which it is our duty to observe carefully.

"As believers of the Word of God, we must learn how to ask God to please accept the free-will-offerings of our mouths — the sacrifices of prayer and praise, which we freely and frequently offer unto Him.

"According to Matthew Henry's Concise Commentary, in 119:105-112, the Word of God, the Bible, directs us in our work and way. And a dark place indeed the world would be without it. The commandment is a lamp kept burning with the oil of the Spirit, as a light to direct us in the choice of our way, and the steps we take in that way."

Meredith leaned in, drinking in the teacher's words.

"The keeping of God's commands here was that of a sinner under a dispensation of mercy, of a believer having part in the covenant of grace. The psalmist is often afflicted, but with a longing to become more holy, he offers up daily prayers for quickening grace."

The instructor continued. "We cannot offer anything to God that He will accept, but what He is pleased to teach us to do. Thank you, Jesus!

"To have our soul or life continually in our hands, implies constant danger of life. Yet he did not forget God's promises, nor his precepts.

"Countless are the snares laid by the wicked, and happy

is that servant of God, whom has not erred from his Master's precepts. Heavenly treasures are a heritage forever. All the saints accept them as such. Therefore, they can be content with little of this world." He let the words settle over the class, waiting briefly for any questions or comments.

"In closing today," the instructor said, "we must look for comfort only in the way of duty, and that duty must be done. A good man, by the grace of God, brings his heart to his work, then it is done well."

The class erupted in a thunderous hand clap and a sense of fulfillment because many in the class were in desperate need of wisdom and direction. By the time the class was over, the needs of understanding were met.

On the way home from work that day, Meredith almost ran to her car and drove over the legal speed limit to get home behind closed doors. In her home, alone with God, she once again set up a private class in her room.

While in her private class, Meredith believed it very special because she was never judged or made a fool of. She could enter without any judgment at all, and she could leave with a greater level of accomplishment and knowledge of her personal walk with God.

Referring back to that day's lesson, Meredith kept rehearsing in her mind, "Thy word is a lamp unto my feet."

As she entered her room and the Lord's presence, she read some thoughts on the passage.

This begins a new portion of the psalm, indicated by the Hebrew letter Nun (נ n), equivalent to our "n." The margin here is "candle." The Hebrew word means a light, lamp or a candle.

The idea is that the Word of God is like a torch or lamp to man in a dark night. It shows him the way—prevents his stumbling over obstacles, falling down precipices, or wandering off into paths which lead into danger or turn him away altogether from the path to life.

"And a light unto my path." The same idea substantially is presented here. It is a light which shines on the road a man treads, so he may see the path, and that he can see any danger which may be in his path. The expression is very beautiful and full of instruction.

He who makes the Word of God his guide and marks its teachings is in the right way. He will clearly see the path. He will be able to mark the road in which he ought to go and to avoid all those by-paths which would lead him astray.

He will see where those by-roads turn off from the main path, often at a very small angle, so there seems to be no divergence.

He will see any obstruction which may lie in his path, any declivity or precipice which may be near, and down which, in a dark night, one might fall. Man needs such a guide, and the Bible is such a guide.

It is important to note for Christians, not only does the Word of God inform us of His will but, it is also a light on a path in darkness. It shows us how to follow the right and avoid the wrong way. The lamp of the Word is not the sun.

It is virtually impossible for mankind to see the Son of God with the naked eye, for it would blind our eyes in our present fallen state. But we may bless God for the light shining in a dark place, to guide us until the Sun of Righteousness shall come, and we shall be made capable of seeing Him.

When Meredith looked at the cross-references of 2 Peter 1:19 and Revelation 22:4, she instantly realized that it was way over her head. Still, she was intrigued to continue on with her studies.

She took a deep breath and grabbed a good snack before diving further into her studies with a strong desire to wrap her brain around the insights of what she believed the verses spoke to her.

The lamp is fed with the oil of the Spirit. The allusion is to the lamps and torches carried at night before an Eastern caravan.

Meredith enjoyed reading different versions of the Bible, so she picked up the Treasury of David, flipped to Psalm 119:105-112, and reads the words aloud.

"Thy word is a lamp unto my feet, and a light unto my path. I have sworn, and I will perform it, that I will keep thy righteous judgments. I am afflicted very much. Quicken me, O Lord, according unto thy word. Accept, I beseech thee, the freewill offerings of my mouth, O Lord, and teach me thy judgments. My soul is continually in my hand, yet do I not forget thy law. The wicked have laid a snare for me: yet I erred not from thy precepts. Thy testimonies have I taken as a heritage forever, for they are the rejoicing of my heart. I have inclined mine heart to perform thy statutes always, even unto the end."

She discovered that we are walkers through the city of this world, and we are often called to go out into its darkness. She thought, let us never venture there without the light-giving Word lest we slip with our feet. She agreed that each man should use the Word of God personally, practically, and habitually, so he might see his way and see what lies in it.

The more that Meredith studied the Bible, the more her spiritual enlightenment brought her into the realm of how she was supposed to be living her life out before men whom she saw daily.

She never would have thought her life would be unfolding in such a manner as it had been when the stranger showed up at her doorsteps, changing the total trajectory of her life as she once knew it.

Prior to that incident, Meredith's life was filled with reports, meetings, more meetings, trips and presentations. She admitted that up until that night, she was pretty much spending every waking hour chasing new ideas, promotions and opportunities to move her company along.

Because of the Bible study, Meredith found herself awakening into a whole new light. Little by little, she put the pieces together of what matters most to God, dimming the spotlight less and less on her business goals and successes.

Instead of being fearful of not having enough or not being totally successful, she realized that when darkness settles all around her, the Word of the Lord, like a flaming torch, reveals her way.

She noted that in the eastern towns, having no fixed lamps in the old times, each passenger carried a lantern with him so he didn't fall into the open poop, or stumble over the heaps of dung which defiled the road.

At that point in her new journey, Meredith was coming into her own, realizing this was totally new territory for her. She needed time to embrace it all. So, for the night, she put her study material down and took a mental break to absorb it all.

She determined to pick it up again in the morning and take one step and one day at a time. She went to bed with the understanding that she didn't have to arrive at the end of her new journey the next day. She could take a breather between steps, and she decided to relax and take it all in.

Continuing on in her personal journey, Meredith realized she also must carry the personal Word of God for her life in her heart and mind, so He continued to lead, guide and direct her every step.

Because this was an important step in her life, Meredith planned to set aside ample time to read, study and meditate upon the Word of God daily. This was a vital part of her new life going forward and quite frankly, she was enjoying it.

On a more personal note, Meredith thought to herself the more she personally dug deeper into her studies that this was a true picture of her path through this dark world.

She understood that up until then, she was trying to carry the weight of her decisions, plans and outcomes for her career and life on her own shoulders.

She never considered there would be another greater option for herself. However, through studying the scriptures, she was finding out that the only way she would know a better way of how to handle things and see it from a different perspective is that she considered walking it out from a different mindset.

Thoughts continued filling her mind. One of the most practical benefits of the Holy Spirit is guidance in the acts of our daily life. It was not sent to astound us with its brilliance, but to guide us by its instruction. True, the head needs illumination, but even more, the feet need direction. Or else, our head and feet may both fall into a ditch.

Meredith was learning every day that happy is the man who personally appropriates God's Word and practically uses it as his comfort and counsellor. Indeed. A lamp to her own feet. "And a light unto my path," she said.

As the Word of God continued drawing her closer to its true purpose for her journey in life, Meredith was constantly reminded that the Word is a lamp by night, a light by day, and a delight at all times.

Through the Book of Psalm, the writer, David guided his own steps by God's Word and also saw the difficulties of his road by its beams. The refreshing thing about David's revelation, to Meredith, was that he always cried out to God and depended upon Him to be his personal compass.

He who walks in darkness is sure, sooner or later, to stumble, while he who walks by the light of day, or by the lamp of night, stumbles not, but keeps his uprightness. "Thank you, Jesus," she whispered.

Ignorance is painful on practical subjects. It breeds indecision and suspense, and these are uncomfortable. The Word of God, by imparting heavenly knowledge, leads to decision, and when that is followed by determined resolution, as in this case, it brings with it great restfulness of heart.

Giving herself a mental break from all the studying and reading, Meredith decided to simply bask in her new discovery and revelation about herself. She opted to just have fun and enjoy the moment.

Meredith heard from her co-workers that they could see a tremendous change in her demeanor. She didn't appear or feel anxious all the time. She took time out to enjoy life more. While she continued to work hard, she was not as work-driven as in years past.

Meredith was very excited and grateful to hear the news from her co-workers. In part, she shared with them that most of it was due to an invitation from Sharon to attend a Bible study group with her.

Still, her team wondered, "Meredith, are you in love with someone special? Are you getting married soon?"

"Who is he?" another asked. "What's his name?"

Meredith looked up with a smirk and simply replied, "Oh, you guys. You'll find out soon enough."

While Meredith hoped one day to live a happily ever-after life with someone very special, more than ever, she knew she had to depend solely upon God to make that happen the right way.

Even though she truly cared about George, and she thought he really cared about her, she wasn't 100% sure anything was possible between the two of them. Perhaps it was merely a fantasy.

The only thing Meredith could think of was how badly she hurt George and how she must have made him feel when she literally screamed at him and ordered him to get out of her house.

As if God was reading her mind, he nudged her. Meredith continued to read Psalm 119:106. "I have sworn, and I will perform it, that I will keep thy righteous judgments"

Under the influence of the clear light of knowledge, David firmly made up his mind and solemnly declared his resolve in the sight of God. Perhaps mistrusting his own fickle mind, he pledged himself in sacred form to abide faithfully to the determinations and decisions of his God.

At that precise moment, it seemed the light bulb came on for Meredith personally. She was intrigued, knowing David resolved that whatever path might open before him, he was sworn to follow the one only upon which the lamp of the Word was shining. She was moved to compassion by his words and his trust in God. Reflecting on it brought tears to her eyes.

She exclaimed, "Wow, what faith in God."

Even though she never witnessed such an incredible faith and longing for the Word of God before, she knew, as she kept reading, that there would be no turning back. She craved more and continued reading.

The Scriptures are God's judgments, or verdicts, upon great moral questions. These are all righteous, and hence righteous men should be resolved to keep them since it must always be right to do right.

Experience shows that the less of covenanting and swearing men formally enter upon, the better. The genius of our Savior's teaching is against all supererogatory pledging and swearing. Yet under the gospel, we ought to feel ourselves as much bound to obey the Word of the Lord as if we had taken an oath to do so.

When a man has vowed, he must be careful to "perform it," and when a man has not vowed in so many words to keep the Lord's judgments, yet is he equally bound to do so by obligations which exist apart from any promise on our part—obligations founded in the eternal fitness of things and confirmed by the abounding goodness of the Lord our God.

Will not every believer own that he is under bonds to the redeeming Lord to follow his example and keep his words? Yes, the vows of the Lord are upon us, especially upon such as have made profession of discipleship, have been baptized into the thrice-holy name, have eaten of the consecrated memorials, and have spoken in the name of the Lord Jesus.

We are enlisted, and sworn in, and are bound to be loyal soldiers all through the war. Thus having taken the word into our hearts by a firm resolve to obey it, we have a lamp within our souls as well as in the Book, and our course will be light unto the end.

On that powerful note, Meredith was so overcome with joy and happiness, she fell back upon her pillows and went straight to sleep.

Somewhere during the midnight hour, Meredith was awakened and felt compelled to ask God for soundness and direction in the inner turmoil that she had shut down at earlier periods in her life.

Feeling the sincere presence of the Holy Spirit hovering over her in that moment, Meredith sat up in bed, stretched out her hands as though she was being given a gift, bowed her head and whispered, "Dear God, please lead, guide and direct me into all of your truths for my life. I welcome you in."

Having taken note of Verse 105 in Psalm 119, she was reminded that it said, "Direct me in all my doubts and difficulties, to preserve from sin and misery, both which often come under the name of darkness, and to comfort me in all my fears and distresses."

Quietly, in her spirit, Meredith heard, "Daughter, My Word is a lamp unto your feet."

This encouraged Meredith that it is a duty both toward God and man. As she meditated, thoughts continued filling her consciousness.

By the lamp—informs and affirms what righteousness required by God to mankind means. By the light of it, a man sees his own deformity and infirmities, the imperfection of his obedience, and that he needs a better righteousness than his own to justify him in the sight of God.

It is a rule of walk and conversation, directing what to do and how to walk. The Gospel part of the Word is a great and glorious light by which men come to have some knowledge of God in Christ—as a God gracious and mercifulness; of Christ, his person, offices, and grace; of righteousness, salvation, and eternal life by him; and it teaches men to live soberly, righteously, and godly.

The whole Scripture reflects that there is a light shining in a dark place; a lamp or torch to be carried in the hand of a believer, while he passes through this dark world; and is in the present state of imperfection, in which he sees things but darkly.

This is the standard of faith and practice. By the light of this lamp, the difference between true and false doctrine may be discerned; error and immorality may be reproved, and made manifest; the way of truth and godliness, in which a man should walk, is pointed out; and by means of it, he may see and shun the stumbling blocks in his way and escape falling into pits and ditches. It is a good light to walk and work by.

Meredith marveled at the idea of a lamp. In her research, she looked at pictures of ancient lamps, their oil providing fuel that made more sense as she meditated on the lessons from her completed study.

"Remember ye not the former things, neither consider the things of old."
~Isaiah 43:18-19 (KJV)

Therefore if any man [be] in Christ, [he is] a new creature: **old things are passed away; behold,** *all things are become new.*
~2 Corinthians 5:17-21 (KJV)

Positive Identification

One day, Meredith read an article written by Sarah Walton, a stay at home mom of four kids all under the age of nine. She knew Sarah as the author of *Hope for the Hurting*.

Through a decade of trials, this mother learned to walk with Christ while her entire family suffered with Lyme disease. For some reason, Meredith was struck by her openness to share with her audience how the gospel speaks into all areas of our lives and gives hope to our suffering.

Up to that point, Meredith had no real reason to believe she was "suffering" in any way. After all, she was a woman with a brilliant education, a fabulous upward swing career and a prosperous business.

All her life, she prided herself on setting her mind to things that mattered to her and accomplishing those things with hard work and much diligence. Very few things escaped her determined grasp.

Yet, the more she perused Sarah's article, the more she felt personally drawn in. Not understanding why, she pressed into finding out what she was overlooking within herself.

There it was in black and white. At some point during the article, Sarah asked her audience, "Why can't we find fulfillment in ourselves? Because we were created to reflect the glory of God. Since the main goal in seeking an identity outside of Christ is to bring glory to ourselves, we will never find lasting fulfillment apart from him."

Immediately, Meredith felt a lump well up in her throat, and hot stingy tears rolled down her cheek. She tried to fight back the tears, but the more she wiped, the faster they ran.

She tried to shake herself from the feeling welling up inside. She thought up until then that she had it altogether, but apparently not. Especially, she found herself doubting almost everything she sensed was right in her life.

Meredith cried uncontrollably, to the point her eyes began to hurt. When she looked in the mirror, all she could see was her tear-stained face and her red, sad eyes. What's with all of this? Meredith thought.

"God, what is this about? I'm successful and fulfilled with my life. Why am I suddenly so sad? I don't understand where this is coming from. God, what's going on? Please God, help me understand."

Seemingly out of nowhere, the question of Meredith's identity came to mind.

"Where are you tempted to find your identity? Is it in your career, material things, your pedigree, family, money, or your social status? Would you trust Me enough to hold your true worth, value and identity in My hands? Would you still be willing to follow Me wherever I lead you?"

It wasn't exactly a voice, yet in her spirit, Meredith heard the questions clearly.

Ironically, these questions prompted Meredith to probe more into her emotions—how she looked at herself and the things that mattered most to her. She wondered if she had been sending mixed signals or confused messages throughout her journey, causing others to look at her differently, without making the connection.

Determined to push through to the commitment of becoming a well-rounded individual who desired the hand of the Lord over her life, Meredith dug her heels into the Word of God and move full speed ahead with her faith in-tow.

She started with a simple subject. "How Our Identity in Christ Changes Our Lives."

Through her research, Meredith learned to know that our identity is in Christ is one thing, but understanding how that practically changes the way we live is another.

She took the liberty of writing down a few ways understanding our true identity in Christ can greatly impact the way we live our lives.

We no longer chase after the desires of our flesh but instead seek to bring God glory in all areas of our lives.

> *Do not love the world or the things in the world. If anyone loves the world, the love of the Father is not in him. For all that is in the world—the desires of the flesh and the desires of the eyes and pride in possessions—is not from the Father but it is from the world. And the world is passing away along with its desires, but whoever does the will of God abides forever. (1 John 2:15-17 ESV)*

If we are not seeking to find our identity in Christ alone, then we are seeking it in something else. However, when our identity is in the eternal things of Christ, we will not be crushed by our failures and weaknesses, fall into pride from worldly success, or despair over disappointments or tragedy.

We won't get lost seeking the attractive but empty things the world offers, because Christ gives us a stable and eternal hope in a world of unstable hopelessness. There is no other place than Jesus Christ that mankind can depend upon and remain in.

Music to Meredith's ears was this echoing, resounding promise from God. When we seek our true identify in Christ, we no longer fear the future.

Which meant to Meredith, whether she was worldly successful or not. Whether "she" found Mr. Right or not, her status in God would never change or be reduced. He would always love her just the same.

> *For all who are led by the Spirit of God are sons of God. For you did not receive the slavery to fall back into fear, but you have received the Spirit of adoption as sons, by whom we cry, "Abba! Father." (Romans 8:14-15 ESV)*

As Meredith continued to read, the spiritual light bulb was coming on in her mind. If we have peace with God, then we have nothing to fear on this earth. So the question might be then, "How sure are you about the peace you think you have in your relationship with God?" Is it solid, out of sorts, or barely holding on?

Our eternities are secure as adopted sons and daughters of Christ. So we don't need to fear financial collapse, losing our job, getting Ebola or coronavirus, or being ridiculed for our faith.

There is absolutely nothing in this world that can separate us from the true love of Jesus Christ. Of course these things aren't easy or painless, but we can have confidence that our Heavenly Father is sovereign over every moment of our lives and will equip us for every single thing He ordains.

Meredith was beaming from ear to ear as she relished in the fact that He bought us with the blood of His own Son so we could claim our identity in the righteousness of Christ. We can trust that He will provide us with everything else we need in this world. Our identity in Christ has given us direct access to our Heavenly Father, who we can call on with confidence and complete trust.

Looking back over her younger years, Meredith was finally able to admit that in high school, she did suffer a bit with rejection from other students who appeared to be more self-assured or more confident than she felt—at least on the outside.

She knew without a doubt she was extremely smart and loved by her parents and family. However, when it came to the others in her class, she was often heckled and called names like "teacher's pet." She was an A student and always got good grades because she spent the necessary time to do so.

Still, looking back, Meredith had to admit that even in her adult years, she occasionally struggled with some challenges with people simply accepting her for who she was, not for what she possessed.

In those moments, Meredith often felt rejected, inadequate, and questioned her judgment when being introduced outside the scope of where she generally felt comfortable. Every time she stepped outside her comfort zone, it felt like a major leap, filled with doubt.

Years later, here she sat in her room alone, reading what seemed like an open invitation to never feel rejected or unwelcomed again—by God, the Creator of all things. She was overwhelmed as well as intrigued at the same time.

As she continued reading, she was unraveling another fact. We have no need to judge or compare ourselves to others when we seek to please Christ alone, in whom our identity is hidden.

> *One person esteems one day as better than another, while another esteems all days alike. Each one should be fully convinced in his own mind. The one who observes the day, observes it in honor of the Lord.*
> *The one who eats, eats in honor of the Lord, since he gives thanks to God, while the one who abstains, abstains in honor of the Lord and gives thanks to God. For none of us lives to himself, and none of us dies to himself.*
> *For if we live, we live to the Lord, and if we die, we die to the Lord. So then, whether we live or whether we die, we are the Lord's. (Romans 14:5-8 ESV)*

Comparing ourselves to those around us or judging the decisions others make can suck the life right out of us. Biblical convictions are hard and fast truths God has given us in His Word to show us the way to live.

Personal convictions, however, are decisions we make within our own families. They may be right for one family, but wrong for another. It's easy to confuse the two and judge others who have different convictions than ours.

Meredith was quickly learning that this can also create insecurity in our choices due to our desire to please man over God. We must be careful that we are not imposing our personal convictions on others, as if we are godlier than they are. This made her think about how she previously handled things with George.

As she kept reading, she realized we can ask Christ for wisdom in this area of personal convictions, be open to hear and discern another's perspectives without judgement, and then walk in confidence that God is the only one we need to honor and please in these decisions.

Still reflecting about her last conversation and outburst with George, she wondered. Had she not been a little swift to rush to judgment about what she thought of him? Even more, how quickly had she dismissed him from her life because she felt he wasn't the type of man she really wanted as a friend? With less judgement, George would still be in her life.

Ashamed and embarrassed for how upset she became, she simply dismissed him from her presence without really giving him a second chance. Since that moment, Meredith had time to think and reflect on just how out of sorts she was in her ugly attitude toward George. She treated him as though he did not matter at all.

Quietly, she came to the understanding that she misjudged George based upon her expectations of how she "thought" he should have represented himself according to Meredith's world.

The other way we compare ourselves is to the giftings and blessings of others. We are all created with the purpose of glorifying God, but in the unique ways He created us. One person is filled with creativity while another glorifies God with a beautiful voice or unique gift. One person glorifies God as a CEO while another glorifies Him by doing custodial work in the church. And one person glorifies God in the way they seek to raise their family, while another glorifies him in the way they use their singleness to serve him.

We must seek to glorify Christ in the gifts and talents he has uniquely chosen for us and not get lost in the joy-sucking pursuit of being something God never created us to be. Don't miss out on the blessing of serving Christ where you are with what He has chosen for you.

More than ever, Meredith wished she had the opportunity for a do-over with George—from the beginning, when she first laid eyes on him, until that moment. She really enjoyed his company, conversations. He was also easy on the eyes. "Just saying," Meredith said with a smile.

However, she doubted in her heart whether he would ever want to see her again, let alone have dinner or go out to a movie. She had not been very nice to him or treated him fairly. Previously, she had given him the impression he was not her "type" and wanted nothing further to do with him. She felt horrible about the whole thing.

Knowing she should not be surprised when suffering came as a result of her own doing, there was still room for her to be confident in reaching back out to George. Being genuinely happy to see him again, in the long run, she should sincerely apologize to him, hoping he would accept her apology. Then they could experience God's forgiveness for the both of them.

> *The Spirit himself bears witness with our spirit that we are children of God, and if children, then heirs—heirs of God and fellow heirs with Christ, provided we suffer with him in order that we may also be glorified with him. (Romans 8:16-17 ESV)*

Through her private Bible study reading that night, Meredith was learning a valuable and important lesson about her identity in Christ. She learned that if our identity is in Christ, then we are guaranteed that one day, we will identify with him in his sufferings.

Just as Christ's sufferings were not hopeless and wasted, neither will ours be. Christ's sufferings defeated sin and death, and therefore we identify with him as he uses suffering to put sin to death in us, to make us reflect more of him.

Not only does suffering sanctify us, but it assures us that after suffering with Him for a while, we will one day be glorified with Him. Meredith had to learn that even though she was struggling with her identity in Christ, she was also gaining a greater knowledge about what it meant to follow God in all her ways.

The next day at work, during lunch, Meredith was excited to share with Sharon, by time a close friend, what she had been learning in the Wednesday afternoon Bible study class about identity in Christ.

The friend chimed in as well. "This theme of suffering has been a familiar one for me over the last several years. While I will be the first to say they have been some of the hardest years of my life, I can also say they have been some of my best. Everyone suffers. But can everyone look back at their suffering with thankfulness and joy because of it? Only those with the hope of Christ can do that. There is no good that comes from suffering if we are apart from Christ or think we can do this suffering thing on our own."

By then, another co-worker, Sandra, was walking by and heard the testimony of Sharon and could not help herself in echoing the same sentiments.

She said, "Excuse me for eavesdropping, but I can attest to the truth. The more I let go of what I thought I wanted (despite my attempts to hold on with a white-knuckled grip), the more I have found joy and treasure in what only Christ could have done through the pain he ordained in my life. Suffering gradually changes our earthly perspective into an eternal view."

At that point, unexpectedly, a crowd gathered around the women in the small break room. Several chimed in the apparent open-door discussion. Meredith, and apparently her co-workers, didn't seem to notice that God was changing the atmosphere right before their very eyes.

Someone in the group added, "We can spend our lives fearing pain and suffering, or we can thank God for the times of reprieve. Then we can trust the seasons of suffering to Christ's great purpose in our lives—to identify with and become more like Him."

Meredith chimed in once again, flooding the group with

questions. "Have you been changed by Christ? Where do you find yourself seeking identity outside of Christ? Do you find yourself holding tightly to something, in fear that you'll be lost without it?"

Some murmured, others looked somewhat blank.

She continued. "Sometimes, in God's grace, He allows the very thing we fear losing the most to be taken away to reveal that we have sought our identity in something other than Him.

"As He grows us in understanding that our true identity is in Him, we are then freed to enjoy and glorify Him in the unique ways He created us to carry out His specific plans for our lives." She paused for only a moment. "We should always choose the freedom God has for us to be in our identities for our lives."

As the open discussion continued, input from the group included more confessions and deliverances.

Another co-worker said, "In my flesh, I have gifts that are riddled with pride and imperfection. I have desires that often seek my will more than God's, and I have blessings I'm prone to hold tightly rather than use them for God's glory."

She swallowed hard. "But that is not my identity anymore. I am righteous, holy, loved, and able to bring Christ glory through the gifts and blessings He has given me. Not by anything of my own doing, but by the grace of Jesus Christ."

Needless to say everyone left the unscheduled break room meeting on cloud nine.

Meredith heard one saying out loud, "Praise God that He loves us enough to take our broken, rebellious hearts, and because of the sacrifice of His son, He offers us a new

identity in Christ. Let's not settle for anything less."
She wholeheartedly agreed.

Conclusion

"Have this mind among yourselves, which is yours in Christ Jesus."
~ Philippians 2:5 (ESV)

Follow the Leader

Over time, Meredith's faith and insight into the Word of God continued to grow by spiritual leaps and bounds. She grasped understanding the Word of God more quickly and insightfully than ever before.

She believed this enlightening began happening in her life because she was hungry for God's truth to be made available to her through daily living. Meredith remembered that since the incident that happened to her some time ago left her bewildered and scared, she had truly come a very long way.

Her desire was to grow and become more apparent and alive to her daily walking with the Lord. She no longer wanted to assume she "knew of God" but rather that she belonged to Him personally.

Before long, she found herself leading a women's Bible study group at the corporation as she made time for the Word to be part of her daily work schedule.

No, she did not consider herself to be a "Bible scholar," and truthfully, she didn't need to be. Honestly, the only thing required in this instance was her willingness to be transparent alongside humbleness to be used by God.

Meredith knew those who worked with and for her prior to her new personal journey saw a major difference—in her work, life and balance. She was growing into a well-rounded, less stressful and patient woman who no longer rushed to the judgement of others but instead, looked for the good in all.

In those days, Meredith found herself becoming less anxious about making money and becoming "known" in the corporate world. Instead, she was more excited about the gospel of Jesus Christ.

She realized she was sitting on a gold mine of incredible opportunity to make a major difference. By guiding others to Christ, she helped foster a mindset to always allow God to become their soul focus and main priority.

Meredith was instrumental in utilizing the strength, passion, skillset and knowledge of her young team of women and men to help her corporation be taken to the next level.

Under her influence, the company totally restructured the mission and vision statements and purpose for its existence. She wanted to leave a legacy that would change lives for the better and would foster a positive attitude all over the world.

She fully understood the importance of encouragement and upward mobility. She wanted to start a leadership chapter within her corporation that mentored others, encouraging young men and women to be all God called them to be by believing they were called to live their lives on purpose.

Meredith understood through her personal pitfalls and experiences that it was more important now than ever before to lead by example and to be a conduit for others to tunnel through.

She began setting a set time (i.e. such as lunch breaks,

after-hour classes or even off-site meetings) for others to join the group if they so desired. It was never Meredith's intention to make anyone feel excluded from the classes or for that matter that they were forced in any way to sign up.

In fact, it would be just the opposite. The only prerequisite was that it would be their sole desire to be a part of the classes that were being offered. With the mere fact that the memo was being posted at work, she wanted to stress to all that she did not want anyone to feel as though they did not belong through segmented office meetings and presentations.

After all, Meredith knew all too well the importance of being inclusive, and she did not desire that unwantedness be felt by anyone else—in or out of her classroom. She extended a personal invitation to all, whether they attended the class or not.

Over time, it was interesting to see how Meredith took personal ownership in leading the group study. Not only did she create the weekly Bible study, but she was also present in her determination to make sure each person felt the love, acceptance and fellowshipping in the interaction throughout the classroom.

She conducted the sessions with such compassion, love, honesty and vigor. She asked open-ended questions, and then she waited for the answers from those who willfully participated. She often monitored the ones who constantly sat quietly week after week in the class.

One day during a class session, Meredith openly said, "I am almost ashamed to admit this fact, but I have come to know this is true. Whatever is feeding your mind constantly is what will inevitably become your leader—whether it's good, bad or indifferent.

"It is a fact that if you constantly watch a certain program daily for countless hours, you will find yourself almost sad when you miss an episode or your favorite programing is interrupted by a special news report. If a phone call comes from someone at the time you're viewing, you may see it as a nuisance and simply allow the call to go to voicemail for later."

She paused as several people shifted slightly.

Meredith continued. "Sadly, I have encounter a conversation with someone only to have dismissed their presence standing right in front of me, because I felt that what they were saying wasn't that important as what I was in the middle of.

Instead of asking, 'Can we please finish this conversation later? I have deadlines to meet, but I would love to continue it later.' I stood looking in their direction while they spoke, but my mind was definitely not listening to a word they expressed."

Meredith took a deep breath, pushing down tears that wanted to escape her eyes. "The solemn thought that every one of us has a definite moral character, and that our deeds are not an accidental set of outward actions but flow from an inner fountain, needs to be driven home to our consciences.

For most of the actions of humans are done so mechanically, and reflected on so little by the doers, that the conviction of their having any moral character at all, or of our incurring any responsibility for them, is almost extinct in us. Unless something startles conscience into protest.

"It is this shrouded inner self to which supreme care is

to be directed. All noble ethical teaching concurs in this—a man who seeks to be right must keep, in the sense both of watching and of guarding, his inner self.

"Conduct is more easily regulated than character—and less worth regulating. Control must be exercised at the source if it is to be effectual. The counsel of our first text is commonplace of all wholesome moral teaching since the beginning of the world." She paused again, letting the group digest those thoughts.

"When the Word of God references the phrase 'with all diligence,' it is literally 'above all guarding' and energetically expresses the supremacy of this keeping. It should be the foremost, all-pervading aim of every wise man who would not let his life run to waste.

"This phrase may be turned into more modern language today, meaning 'Guard your character with more carefulness than you would your most precious possessions, for it needs continual watchfulness.'

"That guarding is plainly imposed as necessary by the very constitution of our manhood. Our nature is evidently not a republic, but a monarchy. It is full of blind impulses and hungry desires, which take no heed of any law but their own satisfaction.

"If the reins are thrown on the necks of these untamed horses, they will drag the man to destruction. They are only safe when they are curbed and bitted, and held well in."

Again, Meredith paused, looking across the room at each face, reading their emotions. Satisfied that they all seemed onboard with the teaching, she continued.

"Then, there are tastes and inclinations which need guidance and are plainly meant to be subordinate. The will is to govern all the lower self, and our conscience is to govern the will.

"Unmistakably, there are parts of every man's nature which are meant to serve and parts which are appointed to rule. To let the servants usurp the place of the rulers is to bring about what I call role reversal. 'Princes walking and beggars on horseback' as George Herbert once stated."

Toward the end of her class, Meredith stood up and said, "Let's be very clear today, there is no effectual guarding of our hearts, minds and thoughts unless the guarding is directed by God."

She continued, "The counsel in Proverbs is not merely toothless moral commonplace but is associated, as we discussed earlier, with fatherly advice to 'let thine heart keep my commandments' and to 'trust in the Lord with all thine heart.' Only the heart that so trusts will be safely guarded.

"The inherent weakness of all attempts at self-keeping is that keeper and kept being the same personality. The more we need to be kept, the less able we are to affect it.

"If in the very garrison are traitors, how shall the fortress be defended? If, then, we are to exercise an effectual guard over our characters and control over our natures, we must have an outward standard of right and wrong which shall not be deflected by variations in our temperature.

"We need a fixed light to steer toward, which is stable on the fixed shore, not tossing up and down on our decks. We shall cleanse our way only when we 'take heed thereto, according to the Word.'

"For even God's viceroy within, the sovereign conscience, can be warped, perverted, silenced, and is not immune from the spreading infection of evil. When our conscience turns to God, as a mirror to the sun, it is irradiated and flashes illumination into dark corners, but its power depends on being lit by radiations from the very Light of Life."

Several members of the group nodded in agreement, so Meredith shared more.

"If we are ever to have a command power over the rebellious powers within, we must have God's power breathed into us, giving grip and energy to all the good within, quickening every lofty desire, satisfying every aspiration that seeks after Him, cowing all our evil and being the very self of ourselves."

When Meredith finally came up for air, she discovered she no longer had just a general meeting of a group of men and women studying the Bible. She found that the group was now being conformed into a portal through which the Word of God could be funneled through to the lives of people they knew and loved—those who also might be affected and changed.

In the end, the entire class sat in silence for a moment, as if breathless and being transformed in the stillness. No one wanted to leave that presence.

Some even asked, "Can we please stay a little longer?"

Without a word, Meredith continued to teach from the Holy Spirit guidance.

"We need an outward motivation which will stimulate and stir us to effort. Our wills are lamed for good, and the world has strong charms that appeal to us. If we are not to yield to these, there must be somewhere a stronger motive than any the sorceress world has in its stores that will help us to remain focused and determined to stay on task and not succumb to the tricks of the enemy.

"To the writer of the Book of Proverbs, the name of God bore in it such a motive. For us, the name of Jesus, which is Love, bears a yet mightier appeal, and the motive which lies in His death for us is strong enough. It alone is strong enough to fire our whole selves with enthusiastic, grateful love, which will burn up our laziness, sweep evil out of our hearts, and make us swift and glad to do all that pleases Him.

"If we are to keep our hearts with all diligence, we must be 'kept by the power of God.' That power is not merely to make diversion outside the struggling fortress which may force the besiegers to retreat and give up their effort, but it is to enter in and possess the soul which it wills to defend.

"It is when the enemy sees that our lives have a greater support system through the love, guidance and direction of Jesus Christ, and we are no longer walking in our own strength and basic understanding, the enemy realizes that he cannot continue to dominate our overall he has to give up his relentless siege. It is God in us that is our security. However, there is no keeping by God without faith."

The more Meredith studied the Word of God, the more aware of herself in Christ she became. She marveled at how much the Lord loved her and how desperately she wanted a real relationship with Him—a relationship she needed.

Prior to that moment, she never really gave a lot of thought to following any leader outside the scope of her Mother and Father. They were her one and only role models, and they were just about perfect in her world. She didn't need anyone else to mimic because they set the bar for her to follow high.

As she considered that thought, she came into the realization that wasn't true at all. While she was extremely grateful for her parents, they would not be the only prime examples of leadership she ever needed in her life. She needed something much greater and far more powerful.

Everyone has a particular story, or an individual life example or lifestyle that at times can speak to them in some shape, form or fashion. For Meredith, as she continued to study the Word of God, she chose to look at the life of Peter.

While Peter's life, like everyone else, is not perfect, she quickly discovered that he was an expert in such matters. He had a bitter experience that taught him how soon and surely self-confidence became self-despair.

Thoughts flooded Meredith's mind. That divine Power is exerted for our keeping on condition of trusting ourselves to Him and trusting Him for ourselves. And that condition is no arbitrary one, but is prescribed by the very nature of divine help and of human faith.

If God could keep our souls without our trust in Him, He would. He does keep them as far as is possible. However, for all the choicer blessings of His giving, and especially for that of keeping us free from the domination of our lower selves, there must be faith in us if there is to be God's help.

The hand that lays hold on God in Christ must be stretched out and must grasp His warm, gentle, and strong hand. Then His tingling touch infuses strength in us.

If the relieving force is victoriously to enter our hearts, we must throw open the gates and welcome it. Faith is but the open door for God's entrance. It has no efficacy in itself any more than a door has, but all its blessedness depends on what it admits into the hidden chambers of the heart.

At the next corporate Bible study, Meredith told her class that she merely wanted to reiterate with all sincerity that there is no noble life without guarding our hearts; there is no effectual guarding unless God guards; and there is no divine guarding unless through our faith.

She continued with that vein of thought. It is vain to preach self-governing and self-keeping. Unless we can tell the beleaguered heart, Psalm 121:5–8 (ESV). "The Lord is your keeper; the Lord is your shade on your right hand. The sun shall not strike you by day, nor the moon by night. The Lord will keep you from all evil; he will keep your life. The Lord will keep your going out and your coming in from this time forth and forevermore."

We do not apprehend nor experience the divine keeping in its most blessed and fullest reality—unless we find it in Jesus. "To him who is able to keep you from stumbling and to present you before his glorious presence without fault and with great joy." (Jude 1:24 NIV)

"Positive and negative are directions that lead to different outcomes. Which direction do you choose?"
~Brenda Murphy~

My How Time Flies...

It had been over a year since Meredith talked to or saw George. After growing tremendously in her personal walk with the Lord, she could see things much clearer than before meeting and interacting with George.

She felt it was time to reach out and clear the air between them, desperately wanting to make things right. She felt horrible about the way she left things the last time she actually saw George.

Eager to share with him the things she was wrong about, Meredith wanted to ask for his forgiveness. Equally, she wanted to share some things with George she learned about herself that hopefully would be reflected in the outward speech and delivery in how she talked and treated other people.

Nervously, she set a timeframe and reached out to George, asking if he would be interested in meeting for coffee at a shop near him—at his convenience, of course. After a few weeks of silence, George agreed to meet. They set the date and time for the next week.

As excited as Meredith was, she was careful not to rehearse their conversation prior to their meeting. She prayed and asked for guidance and direction from the Lord, wanting their meeting to go well. She hoped George could move forward in a positive way from there.

Since their last time together, she realized that on most of those occasions, she could have handled their conversations and interaction a lot better. In other instances, she probably overacted without thinking about her responses to George. No doubt she often reacted or spoke from a knee- jerk reaction with little regard to how it must have made him feel.

Deep down, she truly enjoyed the company and conversations she had with George. She just thought he was being a bit too forward and was not respecting the boundaries she had in place. However, if the truth be told, she never had any male figure in her life that did not simply jump at her beck and call. That, quite frankly, started Meredith in ways that were overwhelming for her. Still, she was eager to see him once again.

On Tuesday, George called the office and confirmed their meeting at the coffee shop after work on Friday.

Meredith, smiling from ear to ear, calmed herself down enough to say, "Yes, I will see you soon."

Meredith arrived first at the coffee shop. About five minutes later, in walked George, tall and handsome as ever. One look at him, and Meredith silently was smitten by his demeanor and personality. She almost forgot his easiness on the eyes. Almost.

As he reached their table, without thinking, Meredith stood to give him a little hug and smile. While George appeared happy to see her, he seemed taken aback by her physical touch. She didn't blame him. After all, their last meeting ended abruptly and not on a positive note.

At first, everything seemed a bit stifled and awkward.

George acted a little unsure about the purpose of the meeting. He allowed Meredith to take the lead for their time together. Coffee ordered, pleasantries out of the way, Meredith took a deep breath and exhaled.

"George," she said, "first and foremost, I asked you to meet with me tonight because I need to sincerely apologize to you for how terrible our last time together was. I must admit, it took everything within me to ask you to meet with me. I would have fully understood if you didn't. However, I am so happy you said yes."

George rested a finger on his lips but remained silent.

Meredith kept going. "I want you to know I was in a different head space at the time, and as more often than not, uncomfortable being around you. I didn't have the full confidence to be in a full-blown relationship. Yet I knew in my heart that I thoroughly enjoyed your company." She leaned forward.

"I realize I must have sent you mixed messages. At other times, I was unsure how to respond and found myself being nervous, anxious and too vulnerable around you. I couldn't allow myself simply to be truthful with you. I did and said things trying to control the 'friendship' so it would be on my personal terms without any regard for your feelings or input."

George leaned back, relaxing slightly.

Meredith pushed down emotions, wanting to stay on track and not lose her courage. "George, if I am totally honest with you, from the first time I laid eyes on you, I felt in my heart you were a good man. A gentle soul. I didn't quite know how to be myself around you."

About that time, the waitress brought their drinks.

Meredith wasn't sure if the interruption helped or not. George still hadn't spoken.

She rushed on. "I was used to running a successful company and having people work for me. I never knew, nor have I ever been in, a real relationship where I had to lead out with my heart and my emotions until I met you. That in itself caused my proverbial walls to go up very quickly.

"In the moment, all I could think about was to go into a mode of self-protection and not let my guard down for any reason. Often times, after we had spent time together, I felt awful about how things were left between us, and I didn't know exactly how to make it right."

Was that an understanding smile crossing George's face? Meredith wasn't sure, but she had to continue.

"Even today, I wasn't really sure if you would ever want to see me again, let alone sit down for a cup of coffee and just enjoy each other's company—simply enjoy the moment we were sharing. Thank you so very much for agreeing to this. It is greatly appreciated."

She blew out a breath, thankful to have all those words finished.

George, taking a sip of his coffee, leaned forward and said, "Thank you, Meredith, for your openness. I was confused about how you felt during several of our unofficial dates and time we spent together." He took another sip. "I indeed liked spending time with you, and I always liked that you were independent, confident—and frankly, attractive."

"Well, if we're being honest, you are quite easy on a lady's eyes."

They both chuckled.

George continued. "From my perspective, I could have

eased back and perhaps not approached you so strongly at first. I didn't allow you space to feel more comfortable. For that, I sincerely apologize too. Please understand, I only want whatever you define as the best for yourself."

He stopped for a moment, licked his lips and finished. "I wish you the best in each of your endeavors, even if that means we never see each other again."

Hearing George say those words was bittersweet for her. Privately she prayed, "Lord, please do not let this be the end of our friendship."

Meredith tried not to smile too much, but at moments, she could not help herself. For the first time, she felt very comfortable and relaxed in George's presence. In her heart, she really didn't particularly want that private moment to end.

During their two-hour conversation, laughing and sharing at the coffee shop, Meredith didn't notice the time passed so quickly.

She started to apologize when George suddenly leaned forward, took her hand and said, "That's okay. You don't have to apologize. I have been waiting for this time and the chance to get together again."

After another couple of minutes went by. They agreed to get together for a movie and dinner two weeks later. Next time, George would pick Meredith up at her home instead of meeting up. She agreed quickly. Noticeably relaxed, she didn't care if she appeared eager for the date. Yes, their date—official this time.

That night, they left the coffee shop, both apparently floating on Cloud 9. Neither knew the other felt the exact same way, but they certainly hoped so.

They each had so much to share with the other but weren't exactly sure how to go about expressing themselves or their feelings. They didn't want to jinx the moment. They didn't want to risk it going awry. And they both chose instead to simply savor their time together.

Suddenly, Meredith felt in her heart she no longer had to walk in fear about anything. God was with her, and He was more than willing to walk her through that process if she would only allow Him to.

She quietly said in her heart, "Lord, I want you to open my heart and take away any fears that lie between George and me. I trust you completely, Lord, to order my steps."

That night, when Meredith went to bed, she got down on her knees and prayed for God to please word her mouth with the right verbiage to express to George what a blessing he had been in her life and that she did not want to lose their friendship.

Suddenly, she was reminded of the scripture readings that she had just studied. "Remember ye not the former things, neither consider the things of old." (Isaiah 43:18-19 KJV) Another one came from 2 Corinthians 5:17-21 (KJV). "Therefore if any man [be] in Christ, [he is] a new creature: **old things are passed away; behold**, all things are become new."

Meredith was reminded not to focus on the old her but rather to accentuate the new, positive, refreshed and revitalized new beginnings of who she became. She was prompted to talk about what God was doing in her life, how her future looked brighter, and how illuminated her path looked day-by-day.

She wanted to share with George how she was growing

in Christ daily and knew more than ever that she was loved and adored by Him forever. It was through His love for her that she could expect great and positive things to happen in her life continuously.

She couldn't wait to see him again. She didn't want to waste any more time apart, never surer about her feelings for George. Her gut was telling her, it's okay—move forward.

For the next couple of days, Meredith could not seem to contain her infectious smile no matter how hard she tried.

People asked her around the office, "Hey, what's up with you? Is there something special going on in your life?"

She in return replied, "Every day with Jesus, is sweeter than the day before!"

On Tuesday, Meredith received a phone call from George asking her out on Friday night to a special place he thought she would like. He explained that he already called ahead and made reservations for two and would like to pick her up at around 7:00 p.m. if that was okay with her.

Thrilled, Meredith said, "Yes, I would love that. Until Friday."

She couldn't understand why she was suddenly nervous, giddy, and acting like a teenager. She made sure everything was just right. Her hair, nails, makeup, outfit. She thought, "What am I doing? This is just a date with an old friend. Well kinda. Oh, wait a minute. Did I just say date?"

Admitting it, this was indeed a real date with George. She made up her mind she was no longer going to pretend she didn't like him or enjoy his company and conversation. She was just going to be open and honest with herself and with George and simply enjoy the evening with someone she had quite frankly grown fond of.

On cue, George arrived on Friday evening around 6:45 p.m. with a large bouquet of two dozen fresh long-stem yellow roses. The look in his eyes when Meredith opened the door said everything.

She could see his heart, emotions, and fondness for her all in one glance, and in that instance, truly Meredith felt the exact same way. She knew from that moment forward, she never wanted to live her life without George being in it.

Standing their proudly with a huge smile on his face. Smelling incredible. Looking extremely handsome. With a beautiful bright smile plastered on her face, Meredith welcomed him into her home with sheer confidence and opened arms.

She stood aside. "Come on in, George, and make yourself at home."

During dinner that night, the atmosphere was totally different. The two of them were noticeably in love, although the actual words had not been uttered between the two. They both knew it. They felt it, and this time they were not going to deny it.

George shared his heart first. After Meredith and he placed their orders, he reach for Meredith's hand and looked deeply into her eyes.

"Meredith, considering that this is our first 'official' date as a couple, I honestly have to admit that from the first day I saw you walk into the room, my heart literally skipped a beat. I was smitten, I was excited, and I was in awe. Maybe I didn't go about everything the right way, perhaps I should have been more upfront from the very beginning instead of holding my true feelings within. But tonight, what I am trying to say, I am so glad that we are here, in this place, together."

They both experienced so much freedom, liberty and peace between them that night in sharing their hearts and love for each other. They gave themselves the freedom just to be themselves. Most importantly, neither wanted to allow any more precious time to be stolen over what was not being said between the two of them.

George did an outstanding job in selecting the restaurant, and Meredith did an incredible job keeping the conversation upbeat, open and drama free. It was an incredible night just being together, and they both felt the special magic in the air and the love flowing between them.

Reminiscing later about the dinner, Meredith thought about specific moments during that time when they both paused and stared into each other's eyes as if to say more, but chose otherwise and allowed the moment to simply be savored and appreciated.

On the way back home, George was careful about every single detail of their time spent together. He shared with Meredith about how he'd looked forward to seeing her again and that he often thought of her a lot when she wasn't around. He wanted to reach out to her but was not sure if that would have been such a great idea. He admitted he never stopped hoping.

Deep down, Meredith was touched and suddenly found herself tearing up at his heartfelt words. In that moment, she felt as though she was being introduced to a completely new George.

He sounded the same, looked the same, but this man driving her home was quickly reflecting the man of her future dreams and possibly husband. She found herself blushing as she turned to stare out the window.

From that day forward, George and Meredith found themselves going out to dinner more. They spent time together on various volunteering projects in their communities. Because of their love for sports, they occasionally went to different sporting events "together" as well. In reality, they were inseparable.

As Meredith continued to enjoy her time spent with George, there was no denying she was smitten with his charm, mannerism, professionalism. Not to mention his incredible insight and love for the Word of God and yes, for Meredith too. No one could deny that any more.

She made it her business to take note of his incredible demeanor and how well he carried himself and cared for others, which further intrigued her. She felt most blessed that God gave her another chance to get this right and to grow.

As much as she adored George, she wanted to be absolutely sure she was not being led by her emotions toward him. More so that she was being led by God, this time giving herself permission to take full ownership of her true feelings for him.

Being completely open and honest with herself, Meredith realized that when she first met George, she was not in the right space or place to truly surrender her will to God. Nor her emotions to an authentic relationship that required more of herself than she was ready to offer up to him or anyone to be honest.

Until that moment in her life, she had not allowed anyone or anything to penetrate the walls of shame, embarrassment, bitterness or open wounds she had carried with her all those years.

She thought she could simply bury them and continue to move forward on her own without anyone else ever knowing or being able to detect her misplaced trust, silent rage and uncontrolled temperament. Not until she came into such close proximity of someone who had secretively stolen her heart and matched her eagerness to be truly loved for who he really was.

Not wanting to admit it, George and she were looking for the same things in relationship—love, kindness and a chance to grow old together.

Building a wonderful and successful corporation still remained an incredible dream for Meredith. However, she didn't necessarily want to do it alone. She realized she needed help, but honestly, in her mind, she couldn't relax enough to trust someone else to help her accomplish that dream.

All of Meredith's younger life, while she was extremely smart, witty, beautiful on the outside and tenacious on the inside, she didn't always encounter individuals who thought she worked hard enough. They accused her that most things were given to her on a silver platter, which was not the truth.

In her younger years, more often than not, it was where she experienced the most pain of rejection. It was where most of the students from high school and college did not always celebrate those things that really mattered to Meredith. They acted as though she didn't deserve them, at times causing Meredith to second-guess her efforts and question her ability to become successful on her own.

Over the months, she rehashed what brought her to the point in her life that she could breathe again and learn to trust Christ in her. It was when she started going to the Bible study class.

The changes happened during the moments of being in a place with other believers who cherished and loved the Word of God as much as she did. That made all the difference in Meredith's life.

From day one, when she first went to class with Sharon, she heard the first lesson coming from the book of Joshua. She was hooked and could never have gone back to the old mindset of thinking and responding to God. Something greater inside of herself was compelling her to move forward at any cost—and moving forward was exactly what she did.

> *And if it seem evil unto you to serve the Lord, choose you this day whom ye will serve; whether the gods which your fathers served that were on the other side of the flood, or the gods of the Amorites, in whose land ye dwell: but as for me and my house, we will serve the Lord. (Joshua 24:15 KJV)*

She smiled to herself, thinking of her reaction to the leader of the Bible study group that day when he asked for open feedback from the attendees. There was quite a bit of various and personal input by those who volunteered to speak. She remembered thinking, "I could never just share openly like that."

Then the leader said of Joshua 24:15-28, "It is essential that the service of God's people be performed with a willing mind. For LOVE is the only genuine principle where all acceptable service of God can be received."

Sitting in her room alone, she bowed her head and simply prayed, "Dear God, please continue to lead, guide and order my steps in you from this time forward. I trust You, and I love You. All I really live for now is Your will for my life—nothing else in this world really matters, Amen!"

Coming up on the second year of their official "dating" anniversary, George asked Meredith to take a short weekend well-planned trip with him. He deliberately chose not to disclose the location or the events taking place during their trip—other than to say he believed she would love it.

The more Meredith tried to guess and drag the excitement out of George, he responded to her questions, "You'll find out in due season."

Finally, the date arrived for their trip together, and Meredith found herself smiling brighter than the sun. She literally could not help herself from smiling from one ear to the other.

She thought to herself, "Wow, could this moment really be happening for me and George?"

Just as she considered pinching herself, she came to a screeching halt and said out loud, "I will not second guess myself. I deserve to be happy and even more so in the Lord."

She continued to pack, whispering a prayer. "God, I do not know what you have in store for me this day, but just knowing that it is coming from you makes me appreciate it in advance."

Within a couple of hours, George picked her up, and they were on their way to the airport. Reaching over to hold Meredith's hand, he made her melt inside.

She screamed out loud, "O' my God, help me hold on to this precious moment!"

As she gazed into his eyes, Meredith realized that for the very first time in her life, she was truly in love. She had never felt this way inside. Prior to dating George, Meredith was theoretically married to her career.

Her work and her ability to grow her business took first place in her life, and she didn't really take time out for true love and romance until she met George. Granted, she had to work through the whole process and drop her guard, allowing herself to experience what real love felt like.

And she knew George felt the exact same way about her. In that moment, she didn't care where he was taking her as long as they were together. Deep in her heart, she was ready for the next chapter in their lives.

Once the crew began the boarding process, George held Meredith close to him and said, "Sweetheart, this is going to be a magical weekend for the both of us that I hope you will never forget. I am honored to be taking this journey with you by my side every step of the way."

On the plane, they chatted for a bit before Meredith drifted off to sleep in George's arms. When she woke, they were landing at the airport in her hometown. By the time Meredith realized what was happening, they were deplaning, and she began to sob with both her hands covering her face.

Once again, George held her close to his chest. "Sweetheart, I sure do hope these are your happy tears! We are simply moving one step closer to what we both want. Are you ready for this?"

She nodded, not trusting her voice.

Arriving at her parents' home, Meredith was mixed with all types of emotions. She was excited, nervous, eager, thrilled, but most of all, extremely happy. She wondered what her parents would think of George. Would they like his personality? Would they be able to tell if he was the one for her?

How would they feel about them just showing up at the house without warning that they were coming? Would George be comfortable around her parents, siblings and meeting other family members for the first time?

Determined to stay in the moment, Meredith refused to allow old insecurities and doubts to sabotage what was standing right in front of her.

She remembered a quote someone once shared with her years earlier. "Reality is the mirror of your thoughts. Choose well what you put in front of you." She never did find the author, but loved the truth of it.

At that moment, Meredith was more than sure that the man who stood before her was exactly what she wanted to see and to share her life with from that day forward.

She not only counted her blessings, but she also knew that to think negatively was like taking a drug that would weaken her. Been there and experienced that. She was fully persuaded that moving forward with the love of her life was the next move for her.

By then, Meredith realized that the trip had taken them to her hometown, the place where she grew up. Probably, George was taking her to ask her parents for her hand in marriage. She didn't exactly know all the specific details, because George had not yet given her a play-by-play down to the minute about all the particulars.

Once they were in the rental car, driving away from the airport, Meredith could not hold back her excitement any longer before asking a litany of questions about what was going on. George smiled and enjoyed every moment of it.

Meredith asked, "Well, can I at least call my mom and

let her know I am in town and we are on our way to see her and my dad?"

What Meredith didn't know was that George had already worked out all the particulars beforehand in terms of asking for Meredith's hand in marriage. As for the dinner that night, plans would be worked out after their arrival.

Unbeknownst to Meredith, over the past six months, George had been actively communicating with her parents via email, phone and FaceTime.

Not only did Meredith's parents know this day was coming, they also knew of George's intentions toward their daughter. George and Meredith's parents had taken care of every minute detail of the trip. They had invited friends, family members, and Meredith's closest sisterhood over for the big announcement.

Fully confident, George looked over at Meredith. "No, let's just go up to the door and ring the doorbell. I think everything else will fall into place."

Doorbell rings, lots of hugs, tears, screams and more hugs later, everyone was overwhelmed and over the top happy for the couple. They loved the fact that Meredith and George were going to make a life together. Meredith's parents, affectionately wanting nothing but the very best for both of them moving forward, ecstatically welcomed George with opened arms.

Hours later, during the party, George wasted no time in asking everyone for their attention. He wanted to make a special toast to Meredith for introducing him to her beautiful family and incredible parents. He also thanked her special friends who had been a blessing to Meredith in ways that mattered the most.

Finally, he saved the very best for last. Bending down on one knee with tears flowing down his face, he looked up at Meredith with an infectious smile.

"Sweetheart, you have no earthly idea how long I have been praying and searching for my soulmate. I honestly have been praying for a spectacular moment, just like this. Now, here you stand. Meredith, would you please do me the honor of saying you will marry me?"

Super excited and overwhelmed at the same time, Meredith could hardly respond. She opened her mouth but was unable to speak. Her heart was overjoyed with love and excitement. She too had been busy praying for an incredible day like this.

Privately, she consistently doubted herself. She knew she had what it took to be successful in business, but was not quite sure she did as a wife. Every time she allowed herself to be remotely happy, she was robbed by the enemy putting negativity in her head.

But that day, standing before the man she loved and adored, her parents and a host of friends and family, she literally screamed, "Yes, yes, yes, George. Yes, I will. I love you so very much!"

With a kiss, the deal was sealed, and the crowd roared with unanimous approval.

Through the next year, Meredith and George planned the wedding of their dreams. They didn't spare the expense of having everything they both hoped for on their special wedding day. In the end, everyone that mattered to them was present or accounted for on their wedding day. They were loved beyond measure, and they both were so thankful and blessed to have found each other. They cherished the joy each of them felt at the moment.

After the wedding reception, they were swept away to their honeymoon in Australia and New Zealand, thereby beginning their new life together, embarking upon a journey that would prayerfully span for years and years to come.

Being married and growing in Christ continuously, Meredith could not help but visit that awful and very frightening moment in her life when a stranger appeared at her front door, demanding entry into her home. She remembered him trying desperately to break in and perhaps steal and even kill her and her dreams.

Even now, just thinking about those horrible moments, tears streaming down her face, her heart beating faster and faster, she stole away into her secret place of prayer with the Lord. "Father, please show me what that moment was all about. Please reveal and release me from this overshadowing terror that overtakes me from time-to-time. I want to live in your daily peace and fulfillment. In the Mighty Name of Jesus, Amen."

After that prayer, Meredith waited patiently for a clear response and direction from the Lord.

Within minutes, she heard Him say, "Meredith, trust my plan and process for the steps I have ordered for your life. Always trust, rely and wait on Me for direction. Never try to go it alone. Trust the process I have in place for you."

As Meredith meditated upon the words, she heard in her heart, she came to the conclusion that life often presents unforeseen bends in the road that can throw us off course.

It's important in the trials and seasons of difficulty that we hold to the course God has placed us on. Learning to trust God's process renews and strengthens you to face the journey ahead.

She bowed her head in gratefulness and whispered, "Lord, I thank You for all you have given me and allowed me to be steward over. May Your grace and favor continue to abound in my life now and forever!"

From that moment forward, Meredith and George vowed to spend their days with time before the Lord first. They wanted God to be the center of their lives, their marriage, their hopes and dreams.

George remembered and shared that when he was very young, his parents instilled in him to "trust in the Lord with all your heart." As an adult, he realized this famous passage from Proverbs 3 contains more than just a general statement about living. Instead, he found that these were steps he needed each day to truly walk with God.

Daily, the couple made it their mission to follow seven steps to make sure they continuously leaned on the Lord.

1. Don't Depend on You

We live in a world where trust must be earned and seems to be in short supply. But Solomon, the famous king who wrote Proverbs, knew that trust is exactly where we must start. "Trust in the Lord with all your heart, and do not lean on your own understanding. (Proverbs 3:5 ESV)

Most of us have faced disappointments, which taught us that we can only depend upon ourselves. But living the life God called us to means unlearning that lesson, which is difficult at best but possible one step at a time. Instead, we're meant to rest in God's understanding.

We may know in our minds that He possesses all wisdom. That is the part that stresses us—the fact that we 'don't know his true plan' bothers us most. "Oh, the depth of the riches of the wisdom and knowledge of God! How unsearchable his judgments, and his paths beyond tracing out!" (Romans 11:33 NIV)

Still, sometimes trusting Him completely like that can be tough. So each day, we must consciously lay aside our own plans and expectations—and surrender to His plans. Also, it is most important that we are honest with God and forthright in our true emotions.

What if we don't feel like we can trust Him like that? That's where step 2 comes in.

2. Cry out to God

Surrendering to God begins with our lips and our thoughts. We need more than a commitment to depend on Him. We need to cry out to Him to show that dependence. "In all your ways acknowledge him, and he will make your paths straight." (Proverbs 3:6 NASB)

When we pray, we admit that His ways are higher than ours. We show that we're leaving our troubles, burdens and dreams in His capable hands. In fact, the Bible promises that when we reach out to Him in prayer, He hears us. "Evening, morning, and noon I cry out in distress, and he hears my voice." (Psalm 55:17 NIV)

We handed the keys of our lives to Him, and we know that He's able to lead us. But in order for that to work, we have to follow the next step.

3. Run from Evil

So much in this world can clutter up our relationship with God. John, the writer of the fourth gospel, describes them as desires of the flesh, lusts of the eyes, and pride in our lives (1 John 2:16). In other words, our blessings can easily become our stumbling blocks when we think of them as what we deserve or what we need to be happy.

Instead, life works best when we remember the true source of our blessings—God—and focus on the things that please Him. "Do not be wise in your own eyes; fear the LORD and shun evil." (Proverbs 3:7 NIV)

Sometimes, the only way to live the life God wants us to live is by separating ourselves from bad influences that keep dragging us down. That works best when we start pursuing something else in their place. "Flee the evil desires of youth, and pursue righteousness, faith, love, and peace, along with those who call on the Lord out of a pure heart." (2 Timothy 2:22 NIV)

Is that easy? Not at all. Fleeing from the evil desires that pull at us means spending a lot of time crying out to God and leaning on Him. But our Creator promises to honor our commitment to Him when we shun evil. "This will bring health to your body and nourishment to your bones." (Proverbs 3:8 NIV)

When we pursue Him, we find life—abundant life. Running from evil and pursuing God doesn't come naturally to most people. Instead, it means we have to make a serious change.

4. Put God First in Your Life

It's easiest to put ourselves first. When something good happens, we want to congratulate ourselves with a reward. When something bad happens, we want to console ourselves or find someone to blame. In other words, we often have a "me-centric" starting place.

When it comes to money, the struggle is even harder. But Solomon, who had great wealth himself, knew his money didn't belong to him. "Honor the LORD with your wealth, with the firstfruits of all your crops; then your barns will be filled to overflowing, and your vats will brim over with new wine." (Proverbs 3:9–10 NIV)

If we can trust God with the first of our wealth, we're truly showing how much we depend on Him. Handing over the first part of our paycheck takes a huge amount of faith after all. But doing so means being God-centric. To get there, though, make sure you follow the next step.

5. Check Yourself by God's Word

Let's be honest. We aren't so good at evaluating ourselves. We go to great lengths excusing our behavior, our actions, and our sins. Who needs a defense attorney when we can pretty much find a reason for any bad thing we do?

The prophet Jeremiah captures this very well. "The heart is deceitful above all things and beyond cure. Who can understand it?" (Jeremiah 17:9 NIV)

If we're ever going to truly trust in God and flee evil, we have to know exactly where we stand. We have to find an objective measure that tells us the truth. And that truth comes from God and His Word.

Of course, that doesn't mean we'll always like what we see or how we see it. "My son, do not despise the LORD's discipline and do not resent his rebuke." (Proverbs 3:11 NIV)

That's right. Sometimes it takes something bad happening or seeing ourselves in a bad light before we finally admit we need to change. And the more we're in the Bible, the more likely this is to happen. "I have hidden your word in my heart that I might not sin against you." (Psalm 119:11 NIV)

When we have Scripture planted firmly in our hearts, God will often use that to deal with us.

6. Listen to the Holy Spirit

When Jesus promised to send the Holy Spirit to the church, He told His disciples that this Counselor would be their spiritual compass or GPS. "But the Counselor, the Holy Spirit, whom the Father will send in my name, will teach you all things and will remind you of everything I have said to you." (John 14:26 CSB)

As we go through our day, this same Holy Spirit guides us too. That means, we don't have to go it alone or hope we're getting it right. No, the Holy Spirit leads us into all truth and protects us. "Guard the good deposit that was entrusted to you—guard it with the help of the Holy Spirit who lives in us." (2 Timothy 1:14 NIV)

After all, the gift of the Holy Spirit to believers reminds us that we can truly follow the next step.

7. Rest in God's Love

When we face a difficult world each day, we can sometimes wonder if God even cares. Why do bad things happen? Where is God when I need Him? Solomon reminds us that God never takes a break or leaves us to fend for ourselves. "Because the LORD disciplines those he loves, as a father the son he delights in." (Proverbs 3:12 NIV)

Even in the midst of turmoil, God sticks with us and

uses those challenges to shape us. When we understand that, our perspective completely flips. No longer do we see our setbacks as failures—we see them as moments when God, as our loving Father, works on us.

And that's exactly why we can trust in the Lord with all our hearts. He cares for us every day. He gives us what we need to thrive. He pours blessing after blessing upon us.

Of course, following each of these daily steps isn't easy. That's why Jesus said we have to deny ourselves and follow Him (Matthew 16:24). Trusting God takes a wholehearted commitment from dawn till dusk. But we're never alone in it. "And surely I am with you always, to the very end of the age." (Matthew 28:20 NIV)

In the end, Meredith came to the conclusion that years earlier on that terrifying night, the person at her front door, demanding entrance into her physical home, was not just an innocent bystander lost in the neighborhood. That being was something much colder, sinister and calculating.

In fact, what Meredith was experiencing for the first time was a spiritual intruder at the front door of her heart and will, demanding a hostage takeover of her mind, body, soul and spirit. The intruder was not simply demanding entry into her physical home, but a radical takeover over of all that mattered most to Meredith. He wanted to gain entry to completely alienate her joy, peace and happiness.

He wanted to eradicate any possible chance of Meredith ever believing that God was able, more than enough, and willing to meet her every need according to His riches in glory.

Meredith realized more than ever that had she not refused the enemy entry into both her physical and spiritual home, her life would have been totally different from that night to the present.

Because of that one special invite from a co-worker who knew and understood the power of prayer and supplication, her entire life changed the total trajectory from that day forward.

She would always be thankful unto God for His great hand upon her life and for His perfect will at the center of her joy. As she looked at her spiritual journey, Meredith saw three major takeaways.

Trusting God became critical. The more she exercised the right to do so, the more her trust grew. She found herself strengthened. She relied upon God to help build her trust muscle through a few exercises.

1. Surrender yourself and all your troubles to God.

When you realize there's supernatural strength available to you from above, then your perspective on life will change. You can move from worry to worship by realizing that God is in control of every circumstance in your life. Let Him be the Master of you and everything in your life. Once you stop trying to do things in your own strength, God takes over and lifts you to new heights.

2. Replace negative thoughts with positive ones.

Your thoughts are extremely powerful, and they can affect things like your mood, your attitude, and yes, even your actions. When you find yourself thinking negative thoughts that bring you down, start thinking about positive scriptures that lift you up. You can do this by committing to memory a favorite scripture. For example, Trust in the Lord with all your heart, and lean not on your own understanding; In all your ways acknowledge Him, And He shall direct your paths. (Proverbs 3:5-6 KJV)

Keep repeating that positive verse out loud, whether this verse or another, until your negative thoughts are replaced with God's peace that transcends all understanding.

3. Ask God to give you the patience to wait on Him.

It's a fact that God will come through for you at just the right moment. He'll never fail you. You need to stay in prayer during these times of waiting, because your faith will be tested. During your trial, ask God to give you patience and to help you trust that He knows what's best for you.

Remember, God is never a second late. He always shows up on time.

Having reached a good place through her journey, Meredith and George lived happily ever after. Okay, honestly, they had trials like everyone else. But with God as the focus on their lives and marriages, they overcame every one of them together. Maybe not happily ever after, but they did live in peace and joy.

"Positive thinking means expecting, believing, and visualizing what you want to achieve. It means seeing in your mind's eye the thing you want, as an accomplished fact."
~Brenda Murphy~

Final Thoughts—Leave All the Details Up To God

I do not know a day that goes by when mankind isn't worrying or overwhelmed by the cares and struggles of this world. I remember hearing the older generation saying things like, "If it ain't one thing, it's another." Or, "It seems as though every time I make two steps forward, it is inevitable that I will have to take at least one step backwards."

It is unfortunate, though, that for many, the cares only swirl or evolve around themselves or those in their particular vortex. Sadly, when trouble finds us, and heaven forbid when it stays longer than we intended it to, it leaves us downtrodden, bewildered and often depleted.

Is God really concerned about all the details of our lives? Does He really know every intricate little piece, every moment of each day in our lives? Yes, you bet He does.

Yes, I believe **God** cares **about the details** in our lives—and he expects us to **care** about them too. **God's** heart for the poor, the widow, the fatherless, and the sick, those who are mourning, comes through over and over in Scripture. **God** expects us to **care** for those who need to be cared for.

Let us not think for one moment that we are in control

of our every move or any facet of life. For we cannot do absolutely anything without his power, direction, input or say so. Yes, we have the power to make decisions. However, the final word always comes via God. For that, I am personally ecstatic.

I believe it is quite difficult for mankind to imagine a MIGHTY God that has the time, takes the time or carves out enough time to lend Himself to such self-absorbed beings as humans. However, one of critical oversights about that statement is that Jesus Christ was God's greatest gift to mankind, and we are Jesus' greatest investments. Therefore, he cares, and he is careful to watch over his personal investment.

Why is God concerned not only about the big things but also the small things in our lives? One reason is because He loves us. If He didn't love us, He wouldn't care what happens to us—and He certainly wouldn't care about the little details that often preoccupy our thoughts or cause us the greatest worry.

I cannot fathom my Great Big God zooming in on an electric bill or monthly house note, or whether my pet, Bandit, has an appointment at the vet next week. Surprisingly enough, He really does. Our God cares about all that matters to us and even those things we should be caring about but may not be aware of period.

In fact, not only does He really care, but oftentimes, it's Him that is reminding us of that appointment. Look around you and take note the next time you are out and about. It may or may not surprise you, but most people are caught up in their own earthly affairs—to the point where they are not mindful of what's in front of them.

The other day, a gentleman almost walked into me, so busy focusing on his phone that even though we came close in proximity, he never wavered from what mattered most to him.

Even when I said, "Oh, excuse me," he never looked up but merely stepped to aside and kept looking at his phone. This poor gentleman was so consumed with the thing he exhibited as total importance to him that nothing else mattered. It was all about him and him alone. Now, it probably wasn't anyone on his phone that he was looking at or listening to. It could have simply been a repeat message for all I know. Sometimes we want to "feel" important and appear busy even when we are not. Regardless of how occupied we become, we should never be so engaged that we ignore others around us—especially those we almost collide with.

Others declare themselves so important that they text and drive and certainly respond back to the texts while driving. A couple months ago, I was on my way home from work and could not understand why the car in front of me continuously veered in and out of the lane.

Because the driver was making me extremely nervous, the next opportunity I had to go around, I did so safely and as quickly as possible. While passing, I could not help but look over in the car to see the problem. When I did so, I saw this woman frantically texting and driving—or should I say controlling the steering with her knees.

Head down, texting, only looking up for a brief moment to see if she was in danger. My heart sunk at the mere thought that someone would actually not only place her life in jeopardy but also countless others on the road that day.

All those people simply trying to make it to where they were headed safely drove in danger because she had to text right then.

It doesn't matter if they are putting other lives at risk, because after all, "This message is important now!" No wonder it is shocking to us that God, who is Lord of Lord and Kings of Kings, would care a second about what we are doing. We are so selfish and self-consumed with ourselves by nature.

Even when we are told by God how much He loves us, we are still trying to figure out for ourselves how we are going to make quality time to "Fit this God over the universe into our busy schedules."

I mean, we are glad that He loves and protects us. But doesn't He know that I have a life? Ahhhh, that would be a resounding yes, since He alone was the One who gave that life to us.

But He does love us, and we know this because He sent His only Son into the world to purchase our salvation. Jesus said, "Even the very hairs of your head are all numbered. So don't be afraid" (Matthew 10:30-31 NIV).

But we know God is concerned about even the smallest things for another reason—His greatness. Listen, God is so great that even the tiniest detail of the universe is under His control.

The most distant galaxy. The slightest seed. Even the minutest sub-atomic particle—everything was created by Him and is under His sovereign control.

God is that great! In Christ, the Bible says, "all things were created—and in him all things hold together" (Colossians 1:16-17 NIV).

Most of all, God is concerned about you and me! If you have never done so, turn to Jesus Christ, and by faith humbly submit your life to Him without delay.

As we saw with the story of Meredith, when we turn our lives over to Jesus, He makes everything turn out for our best.

"God is with you, he is working all things together for good, and he will be with you to the end."

Remember, just like the story in this book, always remember that no matter what your goal is in life, our generous God is in every detail of our lives, and He is concerned about our every move.

References

Last accessed 03/24/2021. Scripture references throughout the book taken from https://www.thebible.org

Brown, D., Jamieson, R, and Fausset, A. 1871. *Jamieson-Fausset-Brown Bible Commentary.* (Ps. 119:105-112)

Pawson, D. 2007. *Unlocking the Bible: A Unique Overview of the Whole Bible.* New York: Harper-Collins Publishers

Walton, Sarah, "Four Ways Our Identity in Christ Changes Our Lives," April 9, 2015, Unlocking the Bible, last accessed March 27, 2021, https://www.unlockingthebible.org/2015/04/four-ways-our-identity-in-christ-changes-our-lives/

Various, Bible Study Tools, last accessed March 27, 2021, https://www.biblestudytools.com

CCSB Web Team. "3 Steps to Learning to Trust God At All Times," Jul 21, 2014, Calvary Chapel South Bay, last accessed March 27, 2021, https://www.ccsouthbay.org/blog/trust-god-always

About the Author

Brenda Murphy is the Founder of Innovative Ministries, Inc., and the author and publisher of six books with several more in progress. Brenda writes from personal experiences and her daily walk with God.

Known for her spiritual wit, depth, and down-to-earth style, Brenda weaves colorful illustrations alongside biblical truth to help audiences find contentment, assuredness and endurance with the Lord. Through Brenda's signature wit and poignant story-telling, audiences are prompted to look beyond their circumstances and life situations to embrace, explore and receive the experiences of God's wonderful grace and mercy in the midst of adversity.

In *Spiritual Intruders*, Brenda departs from her normal writing style, instead using a fictional story to convey biblical truths. But the different writing style in no way lessens her propensity for teaching.

In her personal life and through her intimate walk with Christ, Brenda is discovering that every new day is a glorious fresh gift from God our heavenly Father to live in God-ordained purpose! Brenda truly believes that as sons and daughters of the Most High God, we can be confident, courageous and self-reliant in the fact that Jesus Christ, our Lord, loves us beyond our human comprehension. To prove it, we only need to read the Word of God for ourselves and believe in Him alone to find out just how much He really cares about everything that concerns us.

Brenda Murphy is a captivating and inspirational Christian author and popular conference speaker. She has conducted countless women's conferences and has been invited to speak extensively as a keynote speaker both locally and abroad.

Brenda has served as worship leader, intercessory prayer leader, Sunday school superintendent, counsellor, and life coach, as well as a host for family-life conferences, women's retreats, mother-and-daughter brunches, and single events.

Brenda uniquely weaves her life story and her powerful teaching to create a message of encouragement, hope, and motivation to all. A message that challenges everyone to keep their eyes focused on the real prize, and that is none other than Jesus Christ who is Lord over everything.

Brenda is happily married to the absolute love of her life, Audie, for more than 30 years, and she enjoys resting in the perfect will, purpose, and plan of God for their lives. Currently Brenda and Audie reside in the inspiring city of Fort Worth, Texas, which they proudly call home.

Other Books by Brenda Murphy

- *Had it Not Been for the Lord on Her Side*
- *Raw Faith: The Journey Into Trusting God*
- *Forgetting Former Things: The Power of Letting Go*
- *Cycles: Possessing the Power of Living in Freedom*
- *Living in Purpose: On Your Way to a Greater Identity in Christ*

Works in Progress

- *Necessary Boundaries: Safeguarding Your Personal Space*